TANYUIN ACADEMY STORIES

CARLY STEVENS

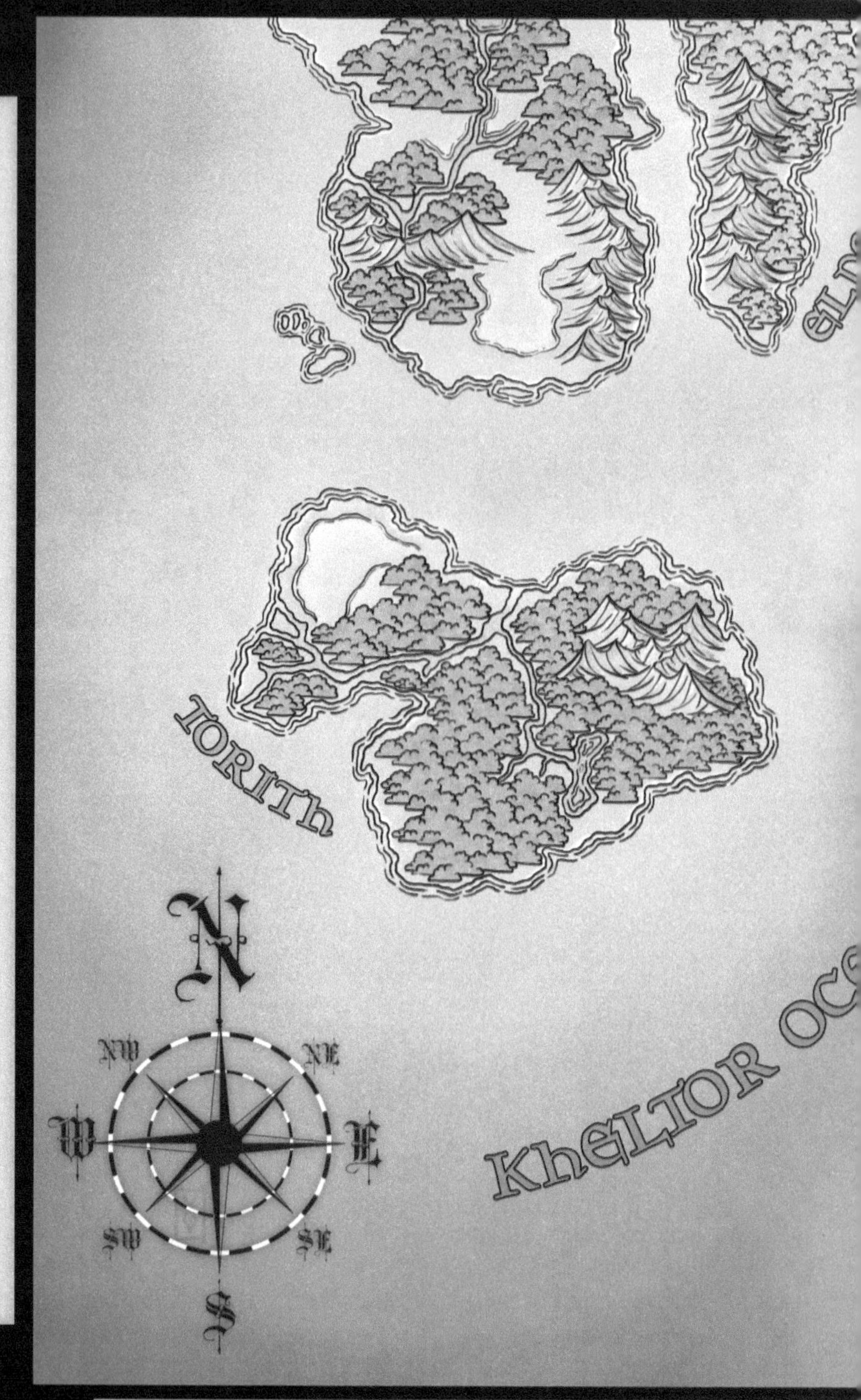
NORITH
KHELTOR OCE
N
NW
NE
W
E
SW
SE
S

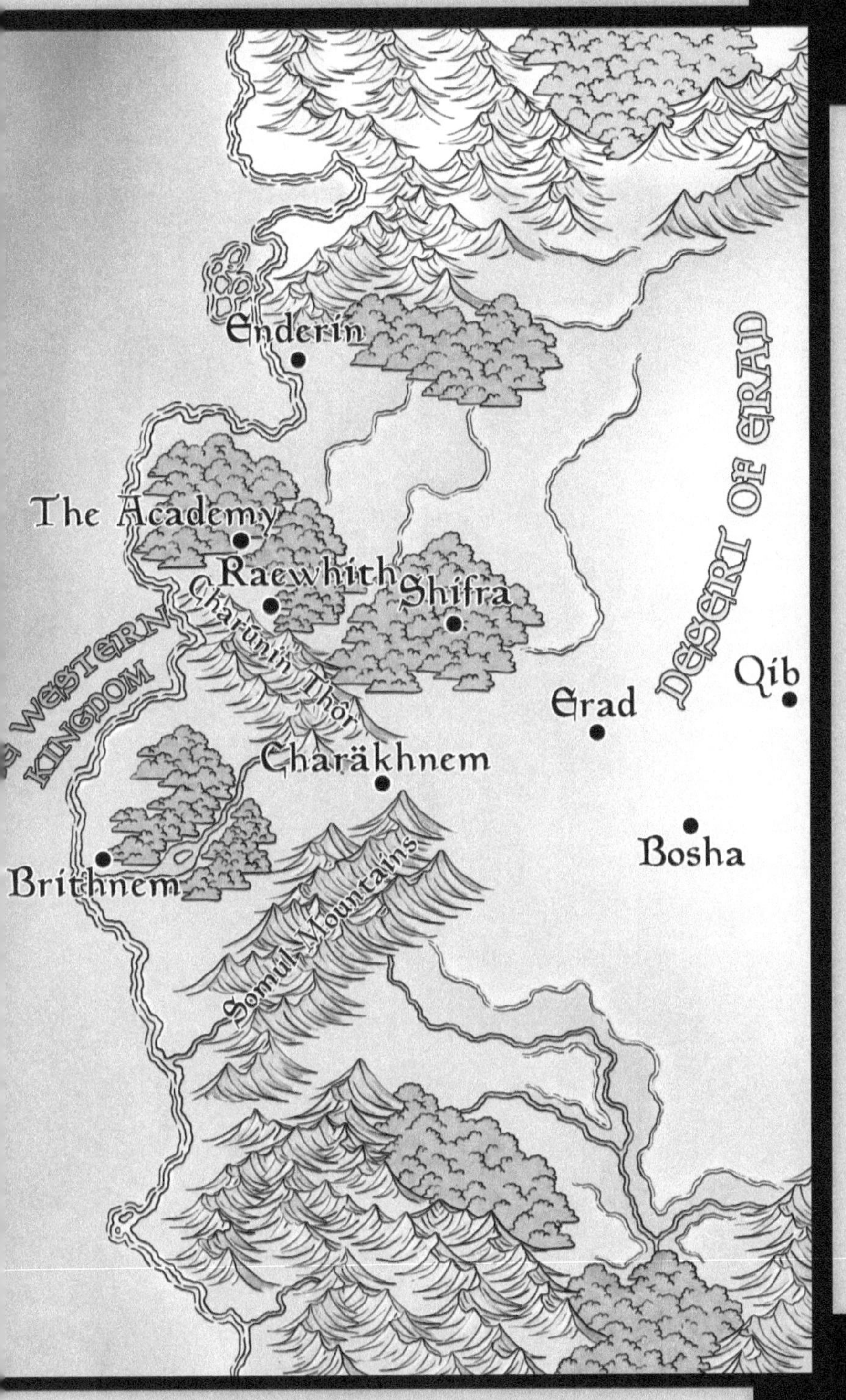

Enderin
The Academy
Raewhith
Shifra
Charúnin Thór
Charäkhnem
Brithnem
Somul Mountains
A Western Kingdom
Desert of Erad
Erad
Qib
Bosha

GR
FORE
GRAND
MARKET SQUA
PORT
amiRan
academy
MON PÁRINATH
R
sho
LITTLE
MARKET

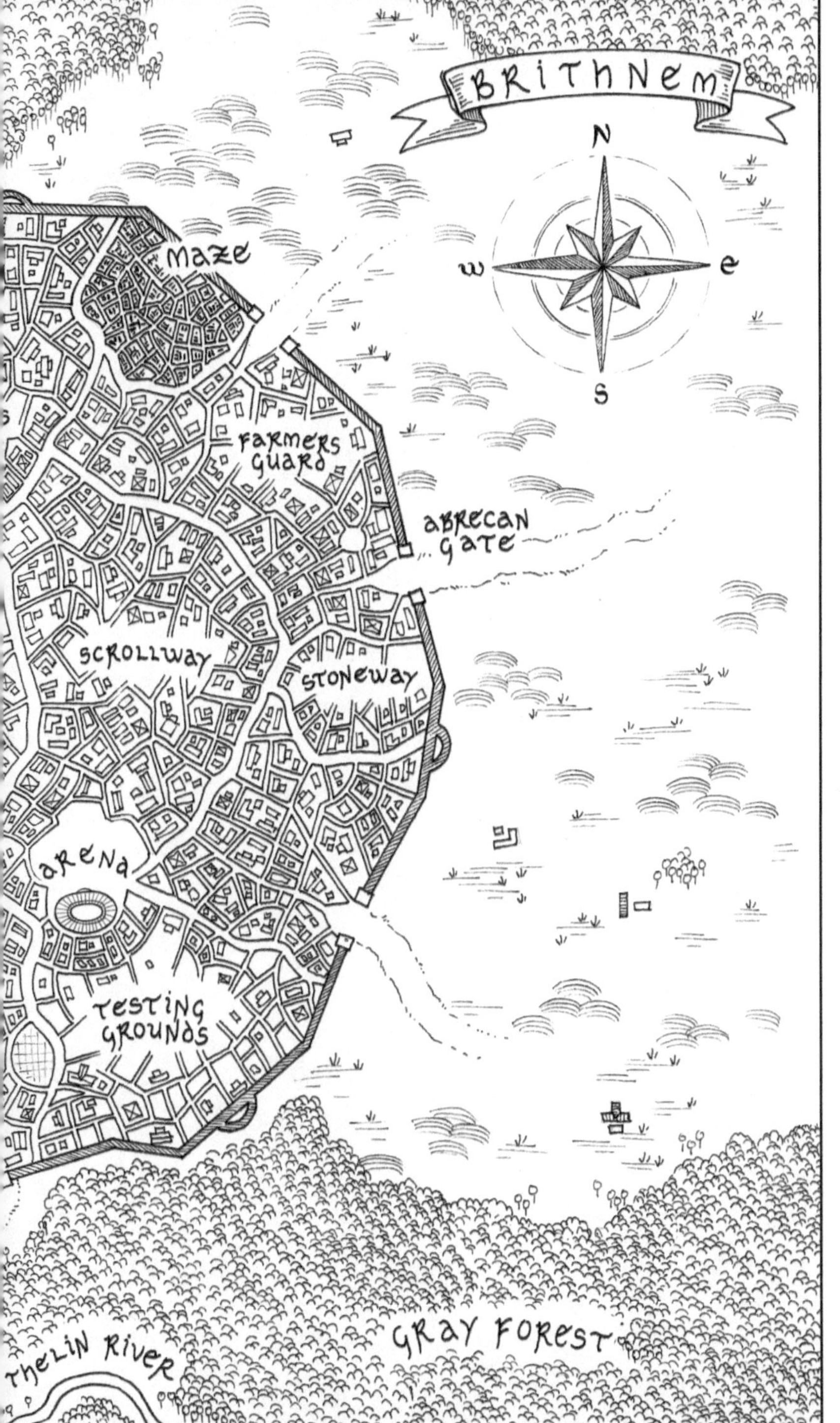

BRITHNEM
N
W
E
S
MAZE
FARMERS GUARD
ABRECAN GATE
SCROLLWAY
STONEWAY
ARENA
TESTING GROUNDS
THELIN RIVER
GRAY FOREST

CONTENTS

1

GHOSTS AND GLASS

FIRIAN KESS HUNG UPSIDE DOWN, shackled to the ceiling. Metal cut into his ankles from the force of his body weight and his rib seared hot with bruises where the highwaymen had punched him, but otherwise he felt calm.

The gang leader, along with his two cronies, looked anything but calm. He purpled with rage, sweat dripping freely down his temples. A bead of it splashed quietly on the stone floor near Firian's head.

Normally, Firian would have come into the thieves' hideout and quietly taken back whatever they had stolen. That, or he would bring them with him for further judgment at the capital. All clear paths that took full advantage of his Academy training.

The problem with this particular situation was that he had found out that morning about the urgent need to distract and capture this gang of thugs. Not much time to plan, and the timing was crucial.

Kiria Arioc would come through this pass soon and the way had to be clear.

A convoy moving across the southern mountains and through the Gray Forest to the capital, carrying coins, currency of the Western Kingdom, and rams, currency of Galve, an up-and-coming trade route city, provided the bait to draw out the thieves. A few hours out from Brithnem, this was by far the most dangerous leg of that journey. Highwaymen regularly murdered and plundered everyone with valuables. They worked in two shifts, either creating a false sense of security or making sure the job was done thoroughly by coming back and killing survivors.

Discovering the thieves' hideout was part of Firian's responsibility too, since so much had gone missing and others had had no luck finding it.

Soldiers of the Western Kingdom planned to sweep up the remaining thieves while Firian occupied the main group. They'd give a signal to let Firian know when it was done.

Instant distraction, finding the hideout, and no time to plan. So he ended up here. Nothing distracted faster than making the enemy think they had the upper hand.

Why no one had told Firian about this until the day of the raid, he wasn't sure. A group of people in the capital still didn't trust him, even after all the good work he'd done the past four years. They probably asked to give him this assignment.

Firian tried out the motion of his wrists. The rope that bound him, tight and rough against his skin, wouldn't come undone, but his hands could move. He let them go limp below his head. His hair swayed gently against his scalp at the movement.

His black Tanyuin shirt bunched around his chest, exposing his midsection. Maybe the thieves had seen that as an invitation to make his stomach and ribs a target.

The purple man widened his stance. Firian tensed his muscles, bracing for a blow. It slammed into him, sending a shot of pain through his already bruised side. He absorbed the punch as best he could, but the force left him swinging nauseatingly back and forth like a pendulum. He grunted and winced, observing what he could while he swung.

The thieves hadn't revealed where they kept all the treasure they'd stolen, but in this cave, or maybe mine, there were plenty of places to start looking. The small entrance hole above ground hadn't revealed that it hid such a cavernous space, with its rough rock walls and cool water smell rising above even the rank odor of the men—one obviously Kingdom with his light skin and dusty brown hair, and two probably Khelê. No Khelê ever looked exactly like another. In this case, one man was tall with long fingers. That was Firian's prevailing impression, his fingers. They looked like they could have pads on the ends of them like a frog. The other was tan and bald with almost no visible ears. His face wasn't ugly, but the lack of ears was distracting. The Kingdom one was in charge, judging by how many of the questions he got to ask.

"Who told you we were here?"

"Who are you?"

"Are you the Ghost?"

That last question was said with a mix of terror and gloating. If these men thought they'd bested the Ghost, they'd have a reason to boast about it. As it turned out, the Ghost was hanging in their lair, but they hadn't bested him.

A horn called in the distance.

Finally.

Firian didn't stir, didn't give away that the trumpet, which sounded exactly like a signal, had been a signal.

The Kingdom man, angry about getting no answers in front of Frog Fingers and Earless, clenched his fists again.

Come closer, just a little closer.

Momentum carried Firian toward him, close enough to strike. Silver glinted at the man's waist. Lashing out, Firian grabbed the key and jabbed his joined fists upward to catch the thief in the jaw.

The two others rushed in as Firian folded in half in mid-air, fighting to unlock the leg irons.

The key wouldn't fit. The quiet but unmistakably teeth-gritting sound of metal against metal rang in his ears as he turned it again, keeping one eye on his opponents. He'd *seen* the man use this key to bind him. Why wasn't it working now?

He focused his attention fully on the irons, briefly but completely. The feel, the sound...

Snick. There it went.

As his legs flung free of their shackles, Academy training took over.

Earless produced a knife. Firian kicked it out of his hands, dropping to the ground so he could catch it. Frog Fingers reached for him, but Firian ducked, threw off his balance, and flipped him with a hard thud on the ground. The little knife worked against the cord still binding his wrists. He flexed against the half-sheared rope. Not yet. A little more.

By this time, the ringleader had recovered, so he and Earless ganged up on him.

The rope snapped and the air felt pure and free around him, a stage for movement. Barely any conscious thought went into the fight, just muscle memory and instinct honed sharp by years.

These men were used to fights, but only against surprised enemies, not Tanyu like Firian. They moved clumsily, relying on their size or fists. Battering rams instead of blades. The Unreal had taught Firian the value of creative maneuvering, and in a few seconds, all three were down, moaning.

Despite the fact that this mission's urgency had been her safety in traveling through this area, Kiria had said not to kill them but to bring them in for judgment.

He hastily tied them up, wrists to ankles, away from anything that they could use to shear the rope away. The rush of the fight waning, he fought not to wince at the pain in his ankles. The place where his feet rubbed against his boots felt sticky with blood.

And he was supposed to be a bodyguard tomorrow.

A smirk spread across his face. His wrists chafed and his ankles screamed as he jumped back through the hole into the bright world above, but Kiria had known he could do this. She had all faith that he would return safely and still be able to accompany her on her diplomatic trip to King's Heights. There was a time when she wouldn't have been so trusting.

He summoned soldiers to come and drag the thieves out of their hiding place. Silver-armored men disappeared down the hole to reappear moments later, lugging the struggling thieves with them. Firian helped pull them out.

They left a couple sentinels there until the cave could be searched. Normally, Firian had to do this bit himself, and it felt almost kingly to delegate.

The thieves, both Firian's group and the secondary one, cursed continually and tried to launch themselves sideways off the horses to run. Their struggle slowed down the whole group of soldiers, so it took four hours to get back to Brithnem, the capital city. Good thing they'd started early.

Firian's blood rushed when he saw the palace in the distance, flags aloft, with the ocean glimmering behind. It was childish, maybe, but he was proud of himself and wanted to see pride in other people's eyes too. His palomino mount, sensing his eagerness, tried to bolt but he reined her in as the group got cleared to go through the main gate and into the city.

The horse's hooves clattered noisily on the pavestones. His head pounded with the noise. A dull headache had settled after they began their ride, probably a consequence of hanging upside down for over an hour.

"I'm going up," he announced. His horse danced underneath him. "The Second Keeper is expecting me."

It was true. It was always true. Through their connection, their *katah,* Kiria could sense when he was close.

Without waiting for permission, he kicked his heels and broke away from the group, speeding up the streets toward the palace. He slowed just before he got in sight of the main door, instead strolling casually up and handing the mare off to a groom.

Mon Párinath rose before him, all carved light stone, facing the rest of the city and then fanning back into two great palace wings that surrounded manicured gardens, the domed Amiran Academy, guard barracks, and private sea ports. Leading up to the main double doors were myriad shallow steps. Firian jogged lightly up. The guards recognized him and let him pass, though one clenched his fist over his sword hilt. Habit.

Firian couldn't blame him after the events four years ago, when he had been nineteen. Only Kiria's untiring work had begun to mend the lines of hatred splitting the Western Kingdom between Tanyu and Amir, and between those for and against her as Keeper.

"Uncle Firian!" The cry rang through the massive palace hall as soon as he stepped inside. A little boy with tan skin and dark curls half-toddled, half-ran toward him with all the recklessness of a four-year-old. Firian swept him up. Crumbs of bread and cheese spilled from his clothes onto Firian's.

"Do not throw him," came his mother's smooth, accented voice. Haved Ganesha, princess of Charäkhnem, walked forward, wearing a wrapped red gown and a serious expression. Behind her came Bard Tanery and the Third Keeper Jori Calthwaite, just come from an early supper, it seemed.

"Fir!" Bard greeted, a wide grin splitting his face. "How'd it go? All good?" He glanced him over as though checking for himself.

"The passage is safe. We're bringing in the thieves now. They were right behind me." Firian's arms itched to toss Atael, usually called Telly, but his mother had told him more than once that her boy was getting too big for that. So he held him in the crook of his arm. Telly's trousers were made of something embroidered that aggravated the raw spot on his wrist, but he held on anyway.

"You're tracking in blood," Jori declared, his glass and metal crown catching the light as he pointed at the floor. As though he'd never done that himself.

Firian glanced behind him. Smudged droplets led back to the door. "I'm fine."

But Bard and Haved looked concerned. "You should have a doctor look at it," Haved said, retrieving her son.

Plenty of times, Firian had been forced to see a doctor—for a broken wrist, deep cuts, plucked molars, sun sickness—but he only went if he absolutely had to. His ankles smarted, but they only needed bandages. "I'll take care of it."

"What happened?" asked Jori eagerly, all pretense gone. "This time you have to tell me. As your Keeper, I demand it. Why are you bleeding? Did you get in a fight with all of them at once?" His gray eyes glittered.

Firian pursed his lips. "Not here." Anybody could be walking by, and Firian was not one to leak the Ghost's secrets.

Jori rubbed his hands together, a lopsided smile on his face. "Shall we go, then? I want to know."

Bard laid a hand on his arm. "He should take care of his injuries first."

Jori sighed dramatically. "Fine, but after!"

"After," Firian agreed.

He surveyed the group of royals before him, backlit by many-paned windows. They were missing one.

Catching his look, Bard said, "She's in a meeting. I'm sure she'll be done soon, yeah?"

Her lavender presence had grown louder in his mind the closer he got to the palace. Now it was like an environment to exist in.

Jori observed his fingernails, false archness returning. "She'll be glad to know you took care of things." It was a thank you. Jori, for all his charisma and many friends, cared unconditionally for a small number of people, as he had proven during the Autumn War that took the life of his brother, Haved's husband, Atty. Kiria was on that list.

When Firian took a step in the direction of the Second Keeper's wing, Telly jumped up and down, looking ready to burst. "Did you bring me anything?"

Firian had brought him a tiny toy boat once, months before, but the child hadn't forgotten.

"Not this time."

"Awwww! But..."

"Hush, Atael," said Haved, who always preferred the boy's full name. "Let him get some rest."

Jori crouched down beside the boy. "He can't bring you something every time. He's on very important business for the Keepers." He tapped the boy's nose with his finger. "Helping us beat the bad guys."

"I want to beat the bad guys!"

"You will. But you have to listen to your mother. She knows how to make you big and strong. And you have to stop calling Firian uncle." Jori jabbed a finger against his own chest, covered in a blue and purple vest. "I'm your uncle."

Telly looked imploringly at Haved.

"You can have two uncles," said Haved, conciliatory.

"Three," Jori corrected, casting a look at Bard.

"Right," she conceded. "Three uncles. Now, it is good for boys to play in the sunlight, so we must get outside while we can." With that, she ushered Telly away.

"Master Kess." A guard from somewhere handed Firian a rag. Looking back, he saw a servant cleaning up the blood trail. He wiped off his shoes before going on. If he moved quickly, maybe he wouldn't bleed on the floors. He jogged the rest of the way. What he needed wasn't rest, it was Kiria.

Potted *sachion* trees and portraits and vases and deep rugs rushed past him. As usual, a cadre of guards stood in front of Kiria's door. Near it, a couple doors down, were his small quarters. He slipped inside.

A bunk and a washbasin sat against opposite walls. On a round blue rug, a sturdy trunk held his clothes. There was a generous window with a view to the gardens, and an emergency door that led, through a slim passage, to Kiria's chambers. She had had this space adjusted for whoever served as her bodyguard. Right now, that was Firian.

He tugged off his boots and ripped the rag in two, hastily wrapping his ankles before putting on his second pair of black boots and going out to stand at attention outside Kiria's door.

The guards dismissed themselves when they saw him. Anyone who was strong enough to be the Tanyuin Head, even for a short time, didn't need so many others to help protect the Keeper. One was enough.

After a few minutes, familiar footsteps sounded through the hall. Kiria, flanked by Royce, the head guard who stepped in whenever Firian was out on missions, rounded the corner. As she normally did in the palace, she donned her Original Beauty, heartrending in its perfection—everything she was as a normal woman, only accentuated, made right. In her hair she wore a pointed crown made of crafted metal and broken glass, remnants of the palace before it was partially destroyed several years ago. Her pale, heart-shaped face bore scars: two deep, vertical red lines. One began at the corner of her bottom lip and disappeared at her chin; the other, near it, on her cheek. The meeting must have been important because she wore one of her favorite diplomatic dresses. The bodice was embroidered in silver designs, a repeating *laird* flower, the Brithnem symbol of peace. Its light blue fabric gathered at the waist and flowed down into a cascading skirt like a waterfall. Soft twists rose over her shoulders in place of sleeves and plunged to expose her back with its large royal tattoo. She caught Firian's eye immediately. This was his favorite part of coming home.

Home.

When had he started to think of Brithnem as home?

"You're back," she said, smiling as she approached.

Royce gave a respectful nod and turned back down the corridor, leaving the two of them alone.

"Yeah. Everything should be safe for your trip tomorrow." He stood soldier-straight.

"Did it go all right?"

"No problems."

A line creased between her eyebrows. He fought back a smile at her concern. "Injuries?" she asked.

He tipped his chin. "Just a little."

She walked past him into her room, inviting him to follow. "Let me see. You never take these things seriously."

He came in, shutting the door behind them, and sat in a chair by the fireplace. Only embers glowed in the hearth now.

She moved around the room gathering supplies, adjusting her dress, making a note. Restless. Almost nervous.

"Are you all right?" he asked. She hadn't seemed anxious in the hall. Her meeting had gone well, judging by her expression. But now she wouldn't settle.

"Fine." She sat across from him, composing her features. A genuinely amused look came over her face. "Now, what did you do to yourself?"

"Nothing." He sighed, taking it back. Why did he resist when he loved her to tend to him? Her hands were so gentle, the thought of them made his stomach swoop.

He pulled off his boots again, with the poorly tied cloth beneath. His bruised ribs protested against the movement. He'd almost forgotten about those. "My ankles are cut," he recited, "bruised rib, chafed wrists." Nobody else would get the same list —what were chafed wrists?—but she could charm him better with her touch.

"They caught you?" she asked, surprised.

"I had to distract them somehow."

Kiria pressed her lips together, almost a smile, and reached into the basket she'd deposited by her chair. She produced a shallow pot full of a poultice that smelled like *sachion* leaves, sharp and fresh and heady. He took a deep breath. So much better than the watery, sweaty smell in the cave.

He unbound the rags and spread them out on the hearth to catch any bleeding.

"Foot up," she commanded, laying a cloth from the basket over her lap.

He obeyed, suddenly aware of how dirty his foot was. That was her favorite dress.

She traced the area around the wound lightly with a finger before applying the poultice. It stung, but not terribly. Her face showed an inordinate amount of concentration, as though she were thinking about something else. Slowly, she rubbed the salve over both his ankles in turn, and then wound fresh cloths tight around them.

His chest ached as he watched her. She shouldn't be doing this, tending to him. There were more experienced people who could fix his cuts. But they'd fallen into a rhythm the past four months. He went on missions. She cared for him when he returned. The first time she'd done it, he had kissed her. The memory stirred in him and he leaned forward, ignoring his protesting rib, and cupped her face with one hand, forcing her to look at him. He pressed his lips gently to hers, twisting them just slightly so they fit her scar. That was her favorite kind of kiss, she'd told him once. But she'd said that about other kisses too. The moment was brief, not heated, but he felt a spark pulse between them as she leaned against his mouth.

She took a deep breath and sat back again. He took his leg off her lap, the bandages secure.

"What's wrong?" he asked again.

"Nothing's wrong. Except for your ribs, and your wrists, you said?" She reached for his hand and pulled up the sleeve to reveal a ring of angry red skin there. "Doesn't look too bad."

"You're not a doctor," he teased.

"And your rib?"

He gingerly lifted his black shirt, unsure if there would be any visible injury. A large purple smudge grazed the skin on his left side.

"Ah!" Kiria exclaimed. "That has to hurt so much! Are you going to be able to come tomorrow? I could always bring Royce." The big blond guard was a seasoned fighter, but he didn't have Firian's versatility.

"No. No, I'll do it." He pulled his shirt down again.

"But—"

"Kiria, I want to."

She met his gaze. Something deep and knowing passed between them. This time she was the one who drew close, careful to avoid his ribs and his wrists. Her mouth was soft against his, her fingers playing in his dark hair, and he stood to press her to him, hands against the bare tattoo at her back.

"Firian," she said when they stopped. Her thumb still stroked the hair around his ear. "I've been thinking. A lot."

His body went on alert. Was this the reason she looked so nervous?

"There are a lot of people who don't like you."

He frowned. "I know. So...?"

"But I know you better. I know that you would give anything for me, *have* given everything for me. You are the man I saw back then, the one I wanted." Her voice was quiet and low as she spoke about their past as teenagers, when he had lusted for power and even compromised her to get it. His life had become atonement for his sins. That she trusted him to be her bodyguard, and afterward to be more than that, meant more than he could articulate.

So where was this conversation going?

"You're not a safe choice," she continued, then laughed and laid her forehead against his chest. He raised his chin to get clear of the points in her crown. Gathering herself, she continued. "I'm doing this terribly. I had planned a whole thing, but I thought you'd want something simpler, just with you and me."

His heart hammered in his chest. She gripped him hard now around the waist, as though she could anchor herself to him.

"Oh! Am I hurting you?"

He had completely forgotten about his ribs. "No. What were you going to say?"

She gave him a quick kiss, almost a distraction, but then her amber eyes softened and she held his gaze for a long moment. His breathing sped up as he waited, waited.

"I love you," she finally said.

Simple words, but they pierced him. He'd known it somewhere inside him, but he hadn't explored that place. Instead, he'd taken their relationship one day at a time, resisting the urge to take it too far, to push her further. She was a Keeper of the Western Kingdom, and he was her weapon.

"Firian. Kess." She said it haltingly as though it were the first time. "I want you to marry me."

His breathing stopped. He'd wanted her, body and mind, for a long time, but hadn't dared to hope. Hope unfulfilled hurt too much, and he'd already been given a second chance. He felt weightless, as though he'd gotten Lost in the Unreal. Was this actually happening?

He wrapped his finger around a lock of her hair, stuck in the time between seconds. He realized he was nodding. After a swift scan of the room—nothing was out of place to indicate that this was anything other than reality—he whispered, deep and ardent, "Yes." He planted a kiss on her forehead. "Yes." On her nose. "Yes." Her lips.

She tugged him nearer, and the world was only the two of them. Black against blue. Keeper and Tanyu. Hands, tongues, lips. Minds connected, a mere thought away.

Once upon a time, he thought he'd destroyed every hope he had of being with her. He was too selfish, too violent, too dangerous.

She pulled away, smiling with unguarded joy.

Swallowing a lump in his throat, he curled hair around her ear, as she had done for him. She closed her eyes at the touch, savoring it. He had never said the words, not aloud, not to anyone. But she had asked him to marry her.

"I love you too." The words were true, so true he felt them echo in his chest, but this still felt more dangerous than his peril that morning.

"I know," she whispered, taking his hand and twining her fingers through his. Her lips twitched and she shook her head. "Dangerous." She said the word as though she couldn't believe she'd done it, asked him of all people. But it had become a term of affection.

"Brave," he responded with mock seriousness, their typical response, code words only they understood.

She laughed, a sound that was music, was home, and kissed him.

2

——————

JUST TO GET A HAIRCUT

"IF YOU STARE into my eyes, you can see yourself in them, very small. Try. Look."

Jori bent forward over his crossed legs, opening his eyes wide and tucking a loose lock of hair behind his ear. The lighting wasn't great in the nook where he sat on a table across from the girl, but she played along. He'd known she was a good one from the moment he had seen her eat a slice of fruit off the end of a knife and then join the wild dancing. There was a recklessness about her, intoxicating as a drink. She was tan and curvy, with straight black hair cut short and dyed lighter at the ends. It might have been pink. Or blonde. The light was bad.

The thin, rickety table creaked and threatened to split as she leaned toward him, squinting. The space was little more than a corner piled with storage. A large scrap of green fabric separated it from the alley. Lantern light pierced through the rips and holes, splashing her clothes like paint. That was an idea. White paint at a dark party... He tucked it away for later. Under the table sat a box. It might have held more supplies for the revelers that roared outside in the cramped streets of the Maze.

Atty will be looking for me.

That thought had to intrude *right now*, didn't it? Jori's brother had actually agreed to come for once. But now they were each having their own fun. Jori had left Atty talking to a small group of people around their age eating some kind of gelatinous treat.

Well, probably not their age. Technically, they weren't supposed to be here. Jori, after all, was fourteen and Atty sixteen. Atty might be allowed, but arbitrary rules stopped Jori from doing everything he wanted. Or they would, if he listened. Besides, not only were there drinking and general wildness, but rumors said that Mag Bernan himself had something to do with this event, which made it dangerous too. Surely there were perks to being the corrupt boss of the Maze, like lots of money to throw good parties?

The girl, Goldie, looked into his eyes. She was short and compact, like a squirrel, all folded up like that. And she smelled nice. A little smoky, hint of fruit...

"I don't see anything," she said.

He saw himself in her brown eyes, tiny and distorted.

"Just keep looking. Closer. Mm hm..." Jori was the one coming closer as he said it, but she didn't pull away.

Then he kissed her. One quick, stolen, there-and-gone kiss on the lips.

Goldie didn't gasp or laugh. Instead, she smiled languorously, as though she'd expected it.

"Ha!" Jori cried, unfolding himself and leaping off the skinny table in one impressively awkward motion. "Come on, you."

He took Goldie's hand and tossed back the green fabric. She followed him back into the light with the drinking and the gambling and the dancing.

It was an inside-outside kind of party that sprawled across a dead-end walkway and leaked into the alleys and surrounding rooms. With the lanterns strung overhead, the sky looked black. But bodies and firelight and the coming summertime made the night pleasantly warm. Perfect for dancing.

"Here, I'll show you a dance," Jori shouted over the din. Even the music, mostly drums, could barely be heard over the riot of talking voices, though the vibrations rumbled under their feet. Jori jumped and skipped for a few beats, then stopped and looked expectantly at Goldie.

The tips of her short hair were green. Not what he remembered. She jumped and skipped too, almost a perfect replica of his moves.

He laughed. "Yes!" Together they started up the raucous dance, nearly colliding into all sorts of people, who huffed and swore as they stepped back. Goldie never lost the self-assured look on her face. Smug, almost. Maybe it came from being an older woman—seventeen-ish.

Jori sped up the dance, both of them getting flushed and laughing and beginning to trip over their own feet and the uneven ground. Goldie fell into him.

"Watch out, darling," he said, setting her right again with a wink. "These people will get the wrong idea. Can't have you throwing yourself at me. I'll get us some water. Do you know where...?" He pointed with both hands in an ambiguous spiral.

"There are drinks over there." She nodded to an open doorway.

Perfect. That was where he'd left Atty a few minutes ago. Should have known the drinks would be with the food. Maybe even spiked punch or something. He gave a business-like nod to Goldie and headed off toward the dark entrance.

Gripping the doorframe and swinging inside, he found Atty standing in a little group, still by the snacks he was eating earlier. His cheeks were flushed as he laughed.

"Having a good time?" Jori said, inserting himself into the conversation. Atty's group, it turned out, looked a little rough.

Jori found himself between a middle-aged man with a scowl and a stick-thin girl. Perhaps the scowl wasn't a permanent feature on the man's face, now that Jori looked closer. That scowl was definitely for him. The skinny girl maneuvered her way back to the man, leaving Jori right next to Atty, which was better anyway. There was something odd, though, about the others. He raised his eyebrows as he cast a searching look around. Two men sat semi-conscious against the walls. Lots of doors off this room. Where did they all lead?

He scratched his eyebrow and rallied from the odd sensation. Nobody seemed to have heard his question, so he asked again.

"So good!" Atty said. The whites of his eyes were redder than usual. Atty didn't usually drink very much. The feeling of unease grew.

"Wonderful, wonderful," Jori said. "Let's get some air." Nodding to the others, "Gentlemen."

Atty brushed him off as soon as they returned outside. "I'm great."

"I'm glad you're having a good time. Let's have some of that good time together." Suddenly, he meant it. Drawing his shoulder-length hair behind his ear, he added, "You finally came with me. Don't make me do this alone! I need my brother to keep me out of trouble."

"Impossible," Atty grunted, but his glassy eyes twinkled. "If Kiria can't do it…"

Kiria was his best friend, Atty excluded. Jori had invited her to come too, but she had grown too sensible for these things. The funnest ones, anyway. Too bad. He'd just tell her all about the fun she missed when they returned to the palace.

"Well, I need you to try," Jori said. "I'm like a wild animal. All the fun is in having somebody to chase me around."

Atty rolled his eyes. "I don't chase you around."

"You absolutely do."

"When have I done that?"

Jori prepared his counting fingers. "All the time! There was—"

"Do you have my drink?"

His attention snapped around to a cute shape with black and green hair. He scooped her in by the waist and kissed her cheek. Good thing the music had quieted somewhat so they could hear each other again or he wouldn't have heard her behind him. "This is Goldie."

Atty frowned in recognition, his eyes sliding in and out of focus. Something was off with him. Was it those cubes he was eating...?

"Goldie?" Atty repeated.

"Yes," Jori said. "I can go back for those drinks."

Goldie's gaze became cat-like in its sly focus. "And you are?" she asked Atty.

"I'm... no one." He looked down, shuffled his feet so he angled away from her, his cheeks rosy in the light.

Jori's attention pinged between his brother, who looked abashed, and Goldie, who stared at him with unnerving intensity. "Atty," Jori snapped. "What did you do? What's going on? Are you two secret lovers or something? If you tell me yes, my head will explode."

"No," Goldie said. "Your name is Atty?" Jori could almost see her putting together the pieces in her head.

"Hm?"

"Short for Atael?"

Atty drew his lips in and bit down on them uncertainly. Then he laughed. His mind seemed like a light—bright, then gone. Worry crawled up Jori's back. It took a lot to make him uneasy but something, *something,* wasn't right.

"Atael Calthwaite!" his brother said in a fit of giggles.

A man who had been smoking with a group of other men in a corner glanced up sharply at the name. He looked about as old as Jori's father, except he had no beard. His brown hair was cropped short. He looked Kingdom, that is, fair-skinned and dark-haired, like Jori. There was nothing particularly distinctive about him besides an air of unassailable confidence. He rose and approached.

"Goldie, who's this?" he asked in a friendly voice, taking the pipe from his lips, but his sharp gray eyes revealed something darker.

Atty smiled at him, eyes vacant.

Jori suddenly felt alone. His heartbeat raced as pieces started to assemble in his mind. Goldie *Bernan*? He grinned at the man. "Wouldn't that be funny!" he exclaimed. "I'm Jori and this is my friend Atilano. Goes by Atty. We get that all the time. But I hear the Keprons are more handsome than we are." He pulled a face and glanced at Goldie to see if it made her laugh. She raised an eyebrow in a halfhearted apology.

"Hm," grunted the man.

"And you are?" Jori prompted.

"Sounds like it's more important who you are. I think you've had your fun. It's time to leave." He popped the pipe back into his mouth. Smoke wreathed up around his face. Had he grown taller in the last minute?

Jori took a step back. "Then we'll just go. Lovely party..."

When Atty moved to join him, the man put a hand on Atty's shoulder. "You can stay for a couple more minutes. Been in that room, have you?" His gaze flicked to the dark doorway that led to the transparent snacks. "Let's go back there."

Alarms sounded in Jori's head. "No!" He relaxed his posture to one of ease. "No no no. We came together, so if I have to leave, then he'll come with me. Right?"

Atty's absent expression cleared for a moment and he looked

up at the man steering him toward the open doorway. "Right," he agreed, shaking the hand off his shoulder. The man would not be swayed.

A voice in Jori's ear said, "We don't care if *you* come, but he can't be here."

He turned to look at Goldie, who gave him a little flirtatious smile. But he didn't feel like flirting anymore. "Why not?" he asked, following Atty.

"Keepers should to leave us alone," she said. "It's not that hard. You're not a Keeper."

Jori's heavy suspicions broke the surface into reality. Mag Bernan, the notorious boss of the Maze, was Goldie's father. Mag Bernan had Atty. What would they do to him?

Behind him, the lively music started up again. Jori entered the dark room with the others. All the sparkliness of the party was fading into long, creepy shadows. They wouldn't hurt Atty, would they? He was heir to the throne of the Western Kingdom. They'd earn a death sentence if they did that.

Something shone in Mag Bernan's hand. A knife!

"What, what?" Jori sputtered, taking halting steps on numb legs toward where Mag Bernan stood next to Atty. "No, no no. No no no. That's not... how this is going to happen, right? You're reasonable. I see that. You just want to have a good time. So we'll get out of here and let you enjoy the party." His smile felt more like a grimace than the real thing.

More people had joined Mag Bernan somehow. Maybe they'd been in this room already, waiting for him. Or was everybody at this party at Mag Bernan's command?

"I would never hurt my guest," he said, displaying the object in his hand. Scissors. Then he lowered his voice, "But I won't put up with royals coming into the Maze whenever they feel like it."

"I'm a royal!" Jori blurted before his brain caught up to his words. "Goldie said it was fine if I came here." In fact, he'd already been plenty of times. He even knew some people by now. None at this party, unfortunately.

"Goldie, hm?" He gestured with his scissors to Atty, who flinched, but his lucidity was wearing off. "It's him I'm more concerned about."

As usual, it didn't matter what Jori did. Atty was the heir, so he had to behave better. Normally, that wasn't too much of a problem for him unless Jori dragged him into trouble. Which he had today. Accidentally. So he would drag him out again. Jori bounced on the balls of his feet, trying to come up with a way to get them out of this.

Mag Bernan continued, brandishing the scissors first at Atty's fine vest, and then at his wavy bronze hair. "We'll just remind him of our thoughts on the Calthwaites."

"No!" Jori cried.

A man nearby laughed at Jori's vehemence.

"No, you can just..." He puffed out his lips in a breath as he gathered his thoughts. "Don't do anything to him. I'll do whatever you want."

"Boy's already going to be in trouble."

Don't I know! Jori pictured his father's disappointed face, seeing the boys the next morning—Atty's hair chopped off and him still high on whatever was in that snack. The plan was to go and return without getting caught. This would get them caught —Atty, at least—and it wasn't a leap to figure out who put him up to it.

"Here, you can humiliate me. Cut it all off." His words came breathless as he demonstrated by picking up a hank of his shoulder-length hair and letting it go. He couldn't believe what he was saying. He loved his hair. It looked so good on him.

"Oh, not his," said Goldie mildly, not seeming to see the severity of the situation. Could anything ruffle her? She returned to his side and ran a hand through his dark waves.

"Thank you, darling," he said. "But yes, mine. You can send a message or whatever you like. To me. And then we'll leave." He shrugged, mustering all the nonchalance he could.

Mag Bernan's attention split between Jori and his daughter. He took his hand off Atty's shoulder. A small surge of relief ran through Jori's veins. He could make this right again. It was just hair.

"You might be right," he said, coming closer with the scissors. They gleamed in the darkness. Wasn't a stretch to imagine the boss of the Maze running Jori through with them, leaving him gasping on the floor in Goldie's arms. But it wasn't Goldie who mattered. It was his brother, whom he'd been so excited to take to this party, only for it to end like this.

Jori cleared his throat and his nerves with it, widening his eyes in Atty's direction in the universal sign for *get out of here!*

Mag Bernan grabbed Jori's hair, slowly but not gently. "You won't tell anyone what happened here, and you'll make sure he doesn't come back, right?"

"Absolutely. No need to worry."

"Wait," said Mag Bernan as he noticed Atty heading toward the exit. "Stop him. Maybe he'll remember this."

One of the boss's goons gripped Atty's upper arm and turned him to face Jori.

Mag Bernan gave a couple practice snips close to Jori's ears. Not once this whole time had he looked anything other than completely self-possessed. He was holding two Keprons against their will, and he didn't seem the least bit concerned. That fact unnerved Jori more than the scissors.

"All right. Cut it off," Jori said, squeezing his eyes shut.

Two hours later, Jori hid in the manicured bushes behind the palace with a barely conscious Atty and a haircut that nearly brought him to tears when he touched it. Patchy, with long sections left intact while other areas were practically shaved to the skin. He was a monster. Impulsively, he hunched his back and clawed his hand, just to try it out, since that would be his life now.

Unless Kiria came soon.

A while ago, Jori had found a servant he knew, the aunt to one of Kiria's serving girls, and begged her to make Kiria meet him in the garden. Secretly, of course. Bring scissors.

"Why do you look like that?" Atty touched some of Jori's lank, remaining hair. His beautiful lost waves...

Jori pushed his hand away. "Just helping you," he muttered, "so you don't have to look like this in front of Father."

Aylmor Calthwaite was a reasonable man, often gone on long diplomatic trips, but he valued appearances. Maybe he'd disown Jori. Who needed him anyway? Atty was the one who mattered. Jori, the second-born, was the troublemaker, the fun one, the expendable one.

Just then, quiet footsteps sounded across the flagstones. "Jori," Kiria said in a loud whisper.

Jori waved one hand above the bush.

Kiria's face appeared near his and she gasped, covering her mouth with both hands. In one, she held sewing scissors. Teeny tiny. "What happened to you?"

"Oh, just thought I'd run off to get this haircut," he remarked, pointing to his ruined head.

Atty lunged at Kiria in a hug.

"Atty, what...?" She whirled on Jori. "What's wrong with him? Where have you been?"

Sometimes she could sound so much like a Keeper. At the moment, though, Jori was glad she wasn't one. She hugged Atty back and slowly sat on the ground with him as she disentangled his arms.

Jori eyed his brother ruefully. "I didn't mean it, let it be known!"

Kiria worried her lip. "Is he okay?"

"He's... fine. Maybe a little drugged."

"Drugged!"

"Or not. Could be all the excitement." But he knew it wasn't true. There had been something in those snacks he ate. Otherwise, he wouldn't look so dopey now. Jori clenched Atty's shoulder and shook it in a show of good-humor.

"You know something's wrong," she accused. "Look at him. Look at you!" She gestured with the scissors.

"Careful, darling. You'll put out an eye." *Though it couldn't make me look any worse. Maybe better. An eyepatch could be mysterious...*

"I assume you asked for scissors because of your hair?"

"Why else?"

"I don't know how to cut hair. You should have called for Candrae or her aunt."

Her aunt. Literally the woman she'd sent to find Kiria for him. He sighed. "You're my only option now, love. Will you help me look like less of a hideous monster, or do we have to keep arguing in the shrubbery?"

Kiria's jaw jutted out in frustration, but she twirled her finger to indicate he should turn around. Soon, the snip-snipping of a proper (or at least, more proper) haircut sounded behind him. "These scissors are hard to work with, but it was either these or the garden shears," she murmured.

"These'll do."

Snip snip. "So...?"

"So we got into a little problem at a party."

"Little problem?"

"Mag Bernan."

The haircut stopped. "No."

"Yes. Keep going."

"Mag Bernan," Atty chimed in. "Great party and then whoosh!"

"I'm glad you got out of there alive!" Kiria exclaimed. "What were you thinking?"

"I didn't know he'd be there," Jori said. "Or that he'd be so dead set on humiliating Calthwaites."

"You won't tell Aylmor, will you?"

"You know I'm a year older than you are, yes? Of course I won't."

Kiria rubbed a hand over his shorn skull. "Less to be vain about, though."

"I'm not vain."

"You're the vainest person I know."

"Am not."

"Atty?" Kiria asked.

"You are," he confirmed.

Jori huffed and fell silent. This was not the time to tease him about his beautiful lost hair. He'd done it in a gesture of selfless goodwill. Couldn't they appreciate that?

But right then Atty was appreciating a caterpillar that had inched onto his finger. Jori had the sudden sensation that he'd pop it into his mouth if someone didn't stop him.

"You had no business taking Atty to a dangerous party," Kiria said, in the tone she used when she wanted to sound like her mother.

"But I can jump off cliffs and eat poison and no one will care?"

"I didn't say that. But Atty is—"

"—the heir," Jori said it with her. He was sick of the word. Sick of the fact that his brother was more important.

He turned, sulking, to look at his brother again. In his glassy-eyed haze, Atty marveled at the creature moving along his finger. Wonder transfigured his expression into something that made Jori want to look closer too. He laid a hand on Atty's knee and leaned to get a better look at the caterpillar. It was green and furry, with red and black splotches along its length.

"Don't move your head."

Jori ignored Kiria's protests. How could moving his head make the situation any worse? "That's a great caterpillar," he said.

"Yes," Atty agreed, staring at it as it moved along on many chubby legs.

It was another hour before Kiria was finished, her knees red and swelling under her nightdress. Jori hadn't noticed she had already been in bed until they all stood up to go back into the palace. He'd been too focused on his hair. Completely gone. Atty was starting to be a little more like his normal self, which was encouraging. He could probably sleep off whatever was in those cubes.

Jori went to his room despondent. He fell into bed, smelling of smoke and bushes and sliced fruit. Goldie really had seemed nice. He ran both hands over his head, now free from any long hair whatsoever. What remained was soft but saddening. He felt the exact shape of his skull.

He must have fallen asleep like that because his arms felt tingly the next morning from being raised all night. *Nothing for it, now.* The sun was up and he had to face the family.

His feet dragged as he washed and changed clothes with the help of his serving boys. They didn't ask questions, but he saw them in their eyes.

He saw Atty first as they headed to breakfast. Bags under his brother's eyes told a woeful tale.

"I'm sorry," Atty began, glancing meaningfully at Jori's shorn head.

"Don't be. It was all my idea." Jori bumped into Atty, who shoved back. They both weaved back to each other across the deep carpet of the corridor. "If we need to blame someone, let's blame *him* or *her*. Though she was kind of delightful. Until all this happened, of course."

"You would say that."

"You're just jealous you didn't meet her first."

They bickered until they got to the formal dining room where their father was waiting. Aylmor, with his perfectly trimmed goatee and expression of manly beneficence, took in his sons when they entered. His lips flattened to see the changes in them overnight.

Kiria already sat at the long table too, alongside her parents. A small pile of green capers sat in a pyramid at the corner of her plate, ready to shove over to Atty, the only one of the three who liked them. Her light brown eyes went big and a little scared.

The boys took their seats by their father, across from Kiria.

"You went out last night, I see," Aylmor said quietly.

"Just to get a haircut," Jori replied with a smile.

3

DANGEROUS CREATURES

Firian couldn't believe what he was seeing. For a split second, he was a boy dreaming of exploration and adventure, not a man secretly planning to destroy slave traders.

Shaggy black bears and mountain cats, larger than any he had ever seen in the woods around the Academy, prowled inside flimsy enclosures surrounded by thuggish guards. Some of the creatures, though huge, looked famished, with fur hanging in clumps over a skeletal frame. In its own pen stalked one more creature Firian couldn't name. It was gray and armored, with huge horns protruding from its forehead like a deer mixed with a bull. Wire-like hairs formed a kind of mustache on the creature, which moved when it huffed and bellowed. Nested among the wide teeth were long, pointed incisors. It moved with a deceptively quick step that suggested it wasn't meant to be domesticated.

Kiria and Bard would love to see this. Maybe he'd show Bard in the Unreal later.

Blank amazement passed over Firian like the shock of bright light before strategies began to line up in his brain. Animal pens and guards covered every entrance to the isolated house, so how did anyone get inside?

If not for the neglected yellow fields around the place, it could have been a lonely farm. At one time, it probably had been. The design was simple—a whitewashed box with a slightly pitched roof, similar to thousands of others in Hinter— but obviously reinforced with extra wood and metal. Gnarled trees dotted the white, stubbly landscape.

Unlike the pirate compound on Torith, which this mission reminded him of at times, this operation wasn't centralized. The meetings, both for sales and planning, happened at a cluster of moving locations. This was the first time Firian had observed this house, but, judging from the extra precautions and the fact that various associates had already mentioned this place, he knew it held great significance for the crooked business.

"All you have to do," Bard had instructed a month ago, "is shut down the slave trade base. Kiria says it threatens the Endrians again. Which is bad, obviously. But the base is in Hinter, so we can't unilaterally take care of its citizens, you know?"

Firian's mouth quirked. "Unilaterally? Are you that much of an Amir now?"

His friend gave a half-shrug in the featureless dark of the Unreal. "I just started studying. No."

"Do you even know what unilaterally means?"

"Do you?" There was laughter in Bard's eyes as he asked.

"One-sided," Firian answered. He had won the game, and Bard squinted in defeat, but he was smiling.

"So, I shut down the base?" Firian asked after Bard told him more about the location.

"Yeah."

"Free any people in there? Take care of the leaders?"

Bard chewed his lip. "If you have to. The main thing is the

base itself, you know? If you make it so that it can't be used for that again, then good. If you have to, though."

Firian nodded solemnly. "Should take longer than usual."

"Well, yeah, of course. It's a bigger job. It's okay if it takes months, as long as it's done. No more infrastructure to keep the business going. And none of it comes back to us."

Because it was such an undertaking, he and Bard spent most of the afternoon going over specifics. Kiria, now the most influential Keeper of the Western Kingdom, had not trusted him with something on this scale yet, even two years into his exile. His skin had hummed with anticipation.

Weeks of reconnaissance and planning had strengthened his resolve to do the job right. He even recognized one of the people the slavers planned to sell. Firian had freed her on Torith. They'd snatched her up again like a fish in a net. The idea made him want to hit something. Someone. The head slaver, Ortu Gurthur, mainly.

Firian didn't see him now, but then, he rarely did. The man stayed well hidden and well defended inside his various bases of operation.

Movement caught Firian's attention. To the left of the house, the head slaver's daughter Viv sat in the crook of a branch, swinging her legs back and forth. Her light brown hair tangled in a matted snarl around her pale face. She had the far-off expression of someone planning an imaginary adventure. The young girl, no more than six or seven, didn't have the Talent. Firian had checked everyone close to Gurthur. Regardless, he recognized the absent look on her face.

She wore an incongruously luxurious fur coat that clashed with her dirt-smudged face, like a waif who'd been taken in by kings. Digging in a pocket, she produced a thin bright ribbon, red as blood, and reached toward a bird's nest on the next highest branch. For a while, she tried to weave it through the twigs and grasses there, like adding a bow to a present.

When she stood on the branch to get a better angle for her project, movement back by the pens caught Firian's eye. A burly man wearing a fur hat and a bow across his back shifted in the shallow snow. His hand absently stroked the sword hilt at his hip as he stared at the girl in the tree. Firian had been watching too, but the quality of the look was as different as heat and cold. The guard leered openly.

Firian searched for the girl's father. This wasn't the first time he'd witnessed this kind of behavior during the many hours of surveillance. He'd seen Gurthur backhand guards for giving looks like that. But the father was the only one who kept the unsavory attention for the little girl at bay. With so many other men in the area, someone else should have the decency to punch this one in the nose, but he seemed to egg on the others to flout the rules of basic dignity with him.

A sharp whistle sounded, and the girl looked back and jumped out of the tree. She approached the guards, who had a low conversation with her in Hinterlander. Their gestures seemed to indicate the house.

Firian gritted his teeth. If a single thing happened to that child, he might not be able to hold himself back from killing them all.

He could do it with one thought. Already he was reaching forward with his mind, picking out the beating hearts and pumping lungs of the armed men, who cast each other sugges-tive glances over the girl's head. The temptation to stop their hearts thrilled through his limbs, cold and prickling as the scratchy grasses beneath him.

But there were several problems with that plan. Ever since the Kingdom attack of the Tanyuin Academy when he'd been the Tanyuin Head, he had resolved not to kill unless it was absolutely necessary. In that instance, he had slaughtered a troop of Kingdom soldiers along with one Tanyu he'd grown up with.

This felt necessary, but the girl was with them too. Also, he didn't want to harm the animals behind them any more than they were already harmed by the slaver's near starvation. Finally, most importantly, he couldn't kill them now without jeopardizing people the girl's father planned to sell. He needed more information before he made a move. Killing the guards would show his hand.

He ground his teeth and stayed silent, flat against the ground, breathing slowly so the fog of his breath would dissipate before it could be seen.

One of the guards unsheathed his weapon and took Viv's hand. The bull creature snorted as a second guard opened the gate to one of the pens.

Firian's muscles tensed. He could run. He could jump the fence and defend the girl. He could—

But Viv looked anything but worried, ambling through the enclosure as though it were a stroll down the street. The gray beast pawed the ground. The guard stiffened and held his weapon tighter, but the girl remained supremely unconcerned.

Firian's brows furrowed. What was this?

Another step and the man started to relax. He even rubbed his thumb over the back of Viv's hand, and Firian felt his face getting hot. When the two reached the door to the house, Viv handed the man over the threshold like someone helping a lady step over a puddle. The door closed, and the girl, alone, returned through the animal pen and out to her tree again.

A faint recollection pinged in the back of Firian's memory. Something about harmony with the natural world... Some kind of Ability like Kiria's Beauty or his Talent. It had been a long time since he'd thought about the Sacred Scroll. One thing was clear. The girl had powers. She was an asset to her father as much as the guards were.

How much money would someone pay for immunity like that? The idea stole his breath. Right now, she was too important to her father and his business. Even a monster like Gurthur couldn't see his daughter as equity, could he? But the answer came clearly before Firian had finished the question.

While the girl played out here in sight of the guards, he would stay. If he had to reveal himself by killing one of them, he'd figure out a new way to complete the mission. He spent the rest of the night thinking about slaves and foreign creatures and dirty guards and especially about the girl and her monstrous father.

OVER THE NEXT TWO MONTHS, winter hardened like ice and Firian found himself in a bar that was tiny, cramped, with many dark corners. He had only ordered a glass of fresh water and one ale, but already he regretted it. He couldn't afford to blur the edges of his mind, even now, at the end of an assignment.

After an assignment.

Normally it didn't take more than a moment to shake off any unwelcome feeling from a job. This time was different.

Today, months of patient work had culminated in a few well-placed fires and well-deserved executions. Firian's job was done. Ortu Gurthur couldn't possibly get his filthy business up and running again for a long time. The frozen waters already inhibited foreign shipping all but four months of the year, and they were deep in the throes of winter now.

Against his better judgment, Firian took another sip of ale. One mug wouldn't make him tipsy. He was being too hard on himself. But wasn't that what made him who he was? If a voice didn't compel him to do more, train better, survive with less than everyone around him, he wouldn't be Firian Kess, the Ghost, previously Head of the Tanyuin Academy. His name wouldn't strike fear into strangers.

Fear was useful in this business for the crown, but it wasn't all he wanted. Not like his last target, who was obsessed with it.

More than once, Firian had positioned himself so he could perform the killing ability on Gurthur. More than once, he'd reached toward the disgusting consciousness. It would have been simple to stop his life. The only thing that made Firian hesitate was the girl, Viv, a wisp of a thing with no evidence of a mother. Though she was quiet, she proved herself spunky and adaptable, lost in her own play and oblivious to her father's evil.

Firian's muscles stiffened at the memory of how Gurthur's lackeys had looked at her.

Not unless you have to, went Bard's voice in his brain.

Firian cursed it. *I had to.*

Without the protection of her father, whom every underling overtly feared, the girl was in serious jeopardy. And there were so many associates. Who would take custody of her once Firian rid the world of her evil father? Someone worse?

The thoughts turned his stomach. He gazed into his drink, tucking himself more deeply into the shadow. It didn't taste like ale from the Old Pub in Tánuil. This one had a sour edge. Not what he needed right now.

As he set the mug down on the table, he caught a whiff of smoke rising from his coat sleeve, which wasn't black, but rough and pale gray to blend in with the locals. *That's right. That was today.* When was the last time he'd slept?

The image of Kiria's face rose unbidden to his mind. Hadn't she asked him a similar question once? Fragments of memory chased each other so often that almost everything seemed threaded through with her. Maybe she'd never asked that at all, but it was probably harmless to imagine that she had. *When was the last time you slept?*

For the first time that night, he realized how straight he was holding his spine, as though he were braced flush against a wall.

"Another?" asked the barkeep in Hinterlander.

Firian shook his head no. He'd picked up enough of the language to hold a child's conversation, maybe. Happily, most of the slavers' meetings were conducted in the common tongue, given the disparate group involved.

A group of monsters.

He relaxed the fist he held tight under the table at the same time he relaxed his spine. Breath felt trapped in his chest. Why couldn't he have just killed the bastard?

His weeks of waiting had finally revealed the way that Gurthur communicated with potential buyers and sellers. It was that network that he had to crush. Bard had left the instructions vague, as he often did. The objective was what mattered.

The way Firian interpreted the command was to permanently stifle communication among major players, free the current group of slaves, destroy infrastructure, and kill those with the will and ability to start up the business again. Or at least discredit them beyond repair. That route was more difficult, less direct.

Firian could be patient, but he'd always favored a direct approach.

He'd thought of everything. Almost. Authorities knew to come for the people Gurthur had planned to sell. Firian had watched as they escaped through an exit he'd created before starting the fire. Everyone was accounted for. Extra blankets and coats awaited them in the snow outside. It wouldn't do for anyone to freeze before they could get to a safe location.

Even the animals would be fine. Someone would corral them. Firian had held himself back from investigating further just to see if the slavers owned even more unknown creatures. Before the job was done, he'd glimpsed from a distance, in a hallway of all places, an enormous, lizard-like creature with protrusions jutting from its shoulder blades. A dragon? Standing as high as a large dog and three times as long, it wasn't as big as his imagination would have made it, but it was larger than any similar animal he'd come across. Maybe enormous enough to eat humans, which was certainly the implied threat.

But the lead slaver himself had escaped. No, not escaped. Firian had let him go.

He hadn't contacted Bard yet to say the job was done.

The door to the bar opened and frigid wind unfurled ahead of the patron. The dark beyond almost seemed to bleed in with it. Instinctively, Firian angled his head down, obscuring his features with the fur hat he wore. The slightly charred smell emanating from his clothes was faint enough that no one would notice unless they came close that he had started fires today.

Another blunder in the making. Firian never should have come to this tavern. He should have followed his usual protocol and left the area immediately, heading back to the Tanyuin Academy. Not this. Lingering on the threshold. Why was he hesitating?

But he knew why.

A loud curse from the direction of the bar snagged his attention. The stranger was ranting in accented common tongue and shaking his head. The pale man didn't look familiar, but there was a wild quality to his attitude that suggested he'd just suffered a sudden unjust calamity. Firian cocked his head to hear more clearly. Another associate? The slaving network was vast enough that Firian had noted all the major players, but didn't know all the grunt workers or buyers on sight.

Yes, the man's weedy voice talked about a fire. Firian's senses prickled.

The pale man pulled off his dark green gloves with a violent tug. "Everyone's scattered, and now I have to track them down. This is not my job. Not my job!" He jabbed a thick finger on the counter.

The barkeep who had talked to Firian moments ago looked back at the man impassively.

"What good are bosses anyway if we have to clean up after them? We didn't deserve this."

At that, Firian allowed himself a little smirk. *Like hell you didn't.*

"I even have to watch his little brat. I'm not her mother. I don't know what the hell he's thinking, running off like this! I'm half thinking of leaving her." He roared with frustration, his white-blond beard trembling with fury. His eyes refocused on the bartender. "Well, do I have to explain it to you like *you're* the little whelp? Unless you can fix all this, turn me into somebody else without this godless luck, I need the strongest drink you have." He pounded on the counter again hard enough that a crack sounded across the bar.

Firian pushed his ale away, fighting the urge to glare under his hat at the man. Nothing to attract attention.

Viv wasn't with the man. Where did he leave her? He wouldn't keep her in this cold, would he? And why had her father left her in his care?

Gurthur didn't care about his daughter. He'd left her and run. Firian's reason for sparing the snake had been unfounded after all. Or had it? Maybe, after everything, confusion had overwhelmed the members of the operation enough to make this man think that he had command of Viv, when really her father was trying to find her now. No, Gurthur kept track of his assets.

The bearded man snatched his drink off the counter with such force that a healthy splash of it fell on the ground as he went to find a seat. Rage rolled off him in waves. He passed Firian's table. Almost before he sat down in the next booth, he'd swallowed his mug and ordered another.

Firian pulled his drink close again, not wanting to look out of place while he waited for the man to finish. At least it shouldn't take long. Gurthur's associate would chug enough ales to scramble his mind, stumble out, and reconnect with Viv again. Knowing he was beset by enemies—the morning had given him ample proof of that—this man would want to stow Viv away safely for when his boss came back. He'd hesitate before harming her, fearing repercussions. Firian had a little time before he really had to worry.

In the end, the man ordered eight drinks in the time it took Firian to finish half of his. Heaving a frustrated sigh, he scowled, put his gloves back on, and headed back out into the cold.

One... two... three... four... five... The footsteps faded.

Firian was out the door, payment strewn on the corner table he'd just left. A wall of cold like water hit him. Blue-black snow and sky filled his vision, scored across in a jagged line by the black outline of mountains. A storm had dumped fresh powder on the ground the night before. Firian took three breaths to let his eyes adjust to the darkness. Boot tracks led away from the little tavern. None of the impressions looked small, which made sense. The bearded man had come alone. So where was Viv?

Firian followed the tracks. A stone's throw ahead of him, only a shadow in the night, lumbered the man from the bar. A running stream of curses ran through Firian's mind as he disappeared deeper into the darkness after him, considering where he might have stowed the girl.

Wet smoke plumed from his mouth with every breath. Cold carried with it an undeniable reality that Firian usually enjoyed, but the cold in Tánuil was nothing like North Hinter. His brain didn't feel like it was freezing along with his limbs, though, as it had through some nights spent watching the slavers' movements.

He took a deep breath of frigid air—slowly in, slowly out. This wasn't his mission, but he couldn't leave this part undone. After everything, Viv felt like his responsibility, the last piece of the puzzle.

A small pounding noise echoed through the quiet. Firian quickened his pace.

"All right!" drawled the now-familiar voice.

Off the footpath leading to the tavern, they approached a small stable. Not for horses, it must have been constructed for some other kind of animal. Goat, maybe?

Firian risked getting closer to his target, who trudged toward the structure. His movements were starting to look messy. *Even better.*

The pounding noise stopped, but Firian hadn't imagined it. Viv was in there.

It was easy to kill men in the dark, and, in this case, somewhat satisfying. The bearded man dropped with four knife wounds in his back.

All was quiet. Firian wiped the dagger on his sleeve, scanning the area for any more people. No one. But there was an extra set of large boot prints leading to and from the main stable door. Firian mouthed a curse. Nothing he couldn't handle, but he should have noticed before. The man had an accomplice.

He had to get Viv out. Whispering could alert someone he didn't want to know of his presence. He'd sneak in around the side.

There was only one row of window openings, covered from the inside by thick fabric, not glass. Tromping to the back of the structure, careful to step in existing footpaths, he sliced a corner of the fabric. It was utterly dark inside. He'd hoped to see the source of the knocking, but couldn't see anything. The gamey scent of animals and hay rose from the opening. It was markedly warmer in there.

Gripping his knife firmly in his fist, which he kept out of sight, he whispered the girl's name.

Nothing. He held the blade tighter, thinking of the larger knife he kept under his cloak. His bare fingers stung with the cold.

"Viv?" he tried again. He didn't know if she spoke the common tongue, so he couldn't launch into an easy explanation of who he was. What would he even say? Compromising, he said, "No danger."

"Who are you?" came a young voice. So she did speak the common tongue. He should have known, given who her father was.

"A friend."

"Are you from my father?"

A moment's hesitation. "Yes."

A tiny noise of relief mixed with irritation rose above the shuffling of the animals within. "You said you wouldn't leave me here very long, but I've been waiting forever. I'm so bored!"

"I'm supposed to take you back to him. Is anyone in there with you?"

"No."

"Then I'm opening the door." He ran back around to the front of the barn and unbolted the latch. Apparently, the man at the tavern had relied on secrecy above security. Weak light from the moon and a few houses in the distance spilled into the inky space.

Viv stood there, ankle-deep in hay, caressing a black and white goat as though it were a prized pet. She wore the fur coat she often sported, but a space gapped between her too-short pants and her shoes.

Deep in the recesses of the little barn, something else

crawled, more serpentine than the goats, with jerky measured movements, an alien glint in its eye. The dragon from the hallway? His heart lurched until he remembered that no animal ever harmed the little girl. In the past weeks, he'd seen her play with creatures that would turn anyone else's blood cold. Now, Firian had no time to goggle. The dragon would have food here, if nothing else, until someone came.

"Come on," he said to the girl, who regarded him with as much wariness as though she were wild herself. The presence of the thing in the shadows didn't seem to alarm her. "Your father's waiting."

This seemed to rouse her.

Once he'd coaxed her out of the barn, they crunched through the snow together, making a wide berth to avoid the sight of the body. Firian's mind spun. It was late, which meant Bard would most likely be finished with all his tasks for the day. He might even be asleep. As Firian walked, the girl at his side, he reached reflexively toward his friend in the Unreal.

"I kidnapped a little girl."

"What?" came Bard's bleary reply. Just a voice, not even a dark face.

"Not kidnapped," Firian revised. "But now I don't know what to do with her."

"Who?"

"She's the head slaver's daughter." He proceeded to explain how the mission had gone, how he'd left the villain alive only for the sake of his young daughter, how he'd heard the man in the tavern, and then now.

Looming black mountains soared ahead of them as they walked. Firian assumed that someone would come for the girl soon. Maybe Gurthur himself worried about her and had deployed all the operatives he could account for to find her.

The Western Kingdom had sent him on many covert

missions and the Tanyuin Academy had crafted him into a weapon, but nothing had addressed what to do when a dangerous man's daughter followed you into the snow.

"You're not the same man who put me in the dark," said Viv, squinting at him as she tripped along. She looked a little worried. "Where is he?"

"He's sick."

"No, he's not."

"He got sick all the sudden. Haven't you ever gotten a stomach ache?"

The girl held her middle thoughtfully, then pouted and looked up at him.

"It's going to be a long journey to meet your father. Where would you like to stay for the night? We'll see him in the morning. He's had a rough day."

"Don't you have a place to stay?" she asked accusingly.

"Yes," he found himself answering, although he had no such thing. He was used to heading toward the Academy after missions, taking opportunities to eat and sleep where they presented themselves, sometimes traveling for a day and a night together without stopping. Children couldn't maintain that pace.

"She's with you now?" Bard asked.

"Yes." Even in the Unreal, it came out as a hiss. Frustration with his situation settled on him like a cloud.

"What can I do?" Bard asked.

The question left Firian wondering why he'd alerted Bard in the first place. Firian tended to work alone, but now his mind was blank and he wanted a second opinion. "Nothing, I guess."

Bard gave a rapid nod, his body now visible. "You can keep her safe. Whatever you do, you're the best one to be with her. You'll figure it out."

Bard's belief in him bolstered his belief in himself. Yes, he could see that Viv stayed out of harm's way. Hadn't he accomplished that with others many times over? His chest loosened.

"You're right. I'll let you know how it goes." And Firian returned fully to the Real, where Viv looked at him skeptically in the darkness.

"You don't look like one of my father's men," she said. Fear ought to have filled her eyes at the prospect. Her father was a scoundrel, but one thing could be said for him—he protected his daughter from understanding the danger she was in because of his business.

"My name's Field," he said easily. One of his aliases.

"Field?"

"I have a spot for us. It isn't far. And then you can see your father in the morning." He couldn't remember making the decision not to return her to her father. It had seemed inevitable from the moment he heard her voice in the barn.

She didn't put up a fight this time. The darkness and the cold pressed, freezing, against their faces. He shoved his hands in his pockets. Immediately after, weight dragged against one forearm. Viv held onto him, tucking her own hand between his arm and his torso. Maybe she was afraid of losing him in the dark. It was a legitimate fear. He didn't often walk in the open, and his tendency was to keep to dark spaces and lose the possibility of prying eyes.

Together they walked toward the only place he could think of that could house them both where their pursuers wouldn't find them. The boathouse lay dark. He imagined he could smell the glacial sea beyond, but maybe that was just the snow and night wind.

Viv's hand felt tiny in the crook of his arm. The walk had taken less than an hour, and she hadn't complained (for which he was grateful) but he still needed to get her to shelter.

He eased open the creaky white door, barely distinguishable

from the snow. This had been one of Firian's hideouts while he did reconnaissance. Rowboats hung horizontally from hooks on the walls, protruding outward like the shelled backs of enormous beetles arranged in rows. Oars had been lashed together in pairs and leaned against one corner. An array of ropes and anchors, spears and sailcloth, lay in piles under oiled pelts meant to keep off the frost.

The unpolished spearheads were the detail that had made him feel comfortable lying low here for a couple nights. No one came on a regular basis. Still, this boathouse belonged to someone, and even in the icy winter weather, they were bound to check on their property eventually.

Firian fished in his pocket for a flint. Viv let go of his arm long enough for him to light a glass lantern on the wall. Blue-edged shadows cast weird figures darting out of corners.

The girl shrank to Firian's side. It was only light and shadow, but he had to admit that the place probably looked unsettling from a child's perspective.

"It's all right." He crouched down to her eye level. "Just sit over there. I'll be right back." With an uncertain look at him, she perched herself on a wooden box near the tarp that covered the spears. Dull glints poked out in the direction of the box. Enemies wouldn't be able to grab the best available weapon in the boathouse as easily with the girl in the way. Even a moment of hesitation worked to Firian's advantage.

Her suspicious expression didn't go away, so he took off his fur hat and handed it to her. "Be right back," he repeated, heading back out into the snow.

The problem with snow was how easily someone could follow their tracks. That disadvantage became an advantage when Firian was alone, following someone else, but now, with this girl, it was a liability. The black sky didn't show signs of snowing again, so he had to do his best to confuse their direction.

Clear as daylight lay the impression of deep boot prints alongside much smaller and lighter ones. When the second person whose prints he'd seen at the barn came to retrieve the girl, it wouldn't take them long to figure out what had happened.

He scuffed out their prints, focusing on the littler ones, and ran in various directions to create confusion. The ruse was far from perfect, but he didn't want to leave the boathouse for long.

No one appeared. No sounds but the creaking of ice and tree. But the hair on the back of his neck prickled. He hurried back to the boathouse and slipped inside. Viv sat there where he'd left her, now wearing his warm fur hat.

"Field! Where did you go?" she asked.

"I had to take care of something."

"I'm hungry."

"And tired, I would think. It's getting late."

"It's not late."

"Yes, it is."

She started to argue with him, but he held up a hand. "Quiet." Cocking his head to listen, he knew his instincts had been right. Someone was here.

Firian was in motion. "In here," he commanded, yanking a small boat off the wall and placing it upside down on the ground, angling it so Viv could crawl underneath.

Life among criminals had taught her not to argue with someone in this mood, apparently, because she did as she was told. The fur hat slid down over her eyes in her haste. "No noise. Don't come out till I get you," he whispered before lowering the boat over her.

Another lantern hissed to life under his flint. By the time the door was unceremoniously jerked open, Firian was already straddling a seat, polishing the dull head of a fishing spear.

"Closed," he grunted in Hinterlander, barely looking up from his task.

A pale, wiry man glared around the space, deep-set eyes resting on the overturned boat. He held a long leash in his palm. On its other end stalked a massive reptilian body on clawed legs. A forked tongue slithered out of its blunted snout. It raised its tethered head as it tasted the air. Quick as a spider, it darted around the man at a new angle, stopped. The tail curled after it, thick and scaled. And from the shoulders, two huge knobs protruded. Something like bone stuck out from both, but the flesh looked swollen and uneven. Broken instead of natural. Muscles coiled around its back, flexing and relaxing like breathing. The tongue slid out again and slitted yellow eyes regarded him.

Firian gauged the distance between himself and the beast that had tracked the girl's scent here. That had to be what happened. The creature had to have a purpose beyond pulverizing or poisoning him. It was too clumsy a weapon, though dangerous in its own right. He rubbed the flat side of the spearhead thoughtfully.

"I'm looking for someone who came in here," the man replied. "A man with a child."

Firian ran through the Hinterlander phrases he knew. Enough, but not for a long conversation when he was trying to pass as a local.

His mind ran back to the hat he'd given the girl. She'd been freezing, yes, but the hat helped to hide his dark hair and pass more easily as someone from North Hinter.

Don't make a sound.

"Child? No."

The man walked closer, his hand straying to his belt. Firian had noticed a knife there earlier. A knife and a dragon—that's what Firian was going to call it, regardless of what it really was.

Unusual, but not insurmountable. He had these fishing spears and the dagger in his boot, for starters. That should do it.

"Maybe they came earlier?"

"Did you see them earlier?" The man's voice had deepened. Time was running out to get rid of him without having to kill him. Firian kept his gaze trained away from the overturned rowboat. Would Viv run out if there were a struggle? Did she recognize this man as a friend? Every moment depended on the discretion of a child. How did he end up in this mess?

Also, he was running out of the ability to converse. "No. I just arrived. Hour? Two hours?" He waved the fishing spear casually in place of a shrug. "Come back later."

"We'll just look around first."

The creature at the end of the lead dashed again in that terribly spiderlike way. This time, it crawled toward Viv's hiding place.

Firian's heartbeat thudded in his chest. Spear still in hand, he stood and walked to the boat, laying his other hand on the hull. "Here to buy?"

"No," growled the man, angling away from him.

The knot in Firian's gut loosened a fraction. "This is a good boat. Look!" He stroked the wood grain with two fingers. "Come look. It's the best boat. Only thirty *perit*. Look! For sailing, you must—"

"We're not shopping!" the man snapped, guiding the dragon along the perimeter. The set of his shoulders had lowered from wariness to mere irritation.

Perfect. Firian adjusted his hold on the spear.

"If you have seen this child," the man persisted, not looking at him, "I'll pay you ten *perit* for information. She's in danger and I want her back."

Under Firian's fingers, the boat shifted with a little scrape. His spine stiffened. Had the man noticed? He didn't register that he'd seen the blunder, but the dragon raised its long neck to peer around as though it sensed something was wrong.

Firian cleared his throat loudly to cover up any other sound. "Generous," he mused. "But no child." Chancing to walk away from the rowboat, he approached the man and the creature. The dragon fascinated and appalled him. In different circumstances, he would enjoy watching it. What had they done to it that it had such horrible deformities? Had they ripped off its wings? More to the point, what could it do to him if he got close enough?

He had to deal with the creature first, then the man.

Teeth and claws. Hopefully those were the only dangers it posed. If its skin were poisonous or something, the man wouldn't merely have it on a leash.

The leash. That could do it...

The rowboat rattled once against the ground. Both man and beast perked up in that direction.

Firian lunged, dropping the spear to rip the lead out of the man's hands. The dragon thrashed like a caught fish, much heavier and stronger than he would have expected for something that size. Its short, bowed legs scuttled beneath it as it reared to be free of the sudden pressure. It launched itself toward Viv's rowboat.

The man left Firian with the dragon and ran toward the boat himself. Firian's gaze dashed across the rest of the boathouse.

Ceiling beams.

The thought came like a bolt of lightning. The dragon twisted toward him again, fast as thinking, but Firian leapt, running up the wall, using boat hulls like steps. The creature jumped. Its front legs hung limp as it rose, undulating snake-like toward him. Wet teeth flashed in the lantern light.

The man reached the rowboat, bent down to raise it off the ground...

Firian pushed off from the wall and angled himself, nearly

flying, through the gap between the roof trusses and the ceiling. Could these beams hold the creature's weight? They had to.

A hissing roar sounded from below as the leash yanked the dragon's neck upward. Tension on the lead allowed Firian to stab the rope through a metal hook in the truss as he jumped down.

The dragon kept thrashing, now on two legs, but it couldn't escape, at least not for a minute.

Firian didn't need a full minute.

He tackled the man, who'd lifted the overturned boat to reveal Viv underneath looking like a bear cub in all that fur. The man grunted and fell beneath Firian's attack.

He grabbed the fishing spear and skewered the center of the man's hand to the ground. A scream of pain ripped through the air. Nearby, the child made an echoing noise. Blood spurted and pooled.

Firian bent close to the man's face. The warmth of his choppy breath hit Firian's ear. "He's looking for a buyer, isn't he?"

The man didn't answer. That was enough of a response.

"Then tell him the Ghost is coming," Firian whispered before whacking the side of his head. The intense eyes rolled back and wincing mouth went slack.

On the other side of the boathouse, the dragon snarled. Firian stood and helped Viv to her feet. He wrapped an arm around her, trying to shelter her from both sights, but it was too late for that. Together, they hurried outside into the cold.

The girl ripped away from him. "Who are you?" she demanded, shaking. "My father didn't send you! I want to go home. You need to take me home right now."

"Look," said Firian, "there are bad men trying to hurt you and I'm going to help you."

Her eyes shone with defiant fear in the lingering light of the boathouse. For a second, he thought she might run.

"I'll make sure you're safe."

"You're a bad man." The words were clear but quiet, as though she wasn't quite sure she wanted him to hear them.

"Maybe," he said distractedly, scanning the area.

Her face scrunched with anger, and she looked away, but she didn't bolt. That was all he needed. As long as she didn't run, he could find someplace to get her to safety.

Snow bunched up around their boots as they stood there. He drummed his fingers once against his leg, his decision made. "Come on. You step where I step."

Viv's father was sure to send more cronies after them soon. It might be after first light, but by then, the two of them would be far enough away that they wouldn't be caught. Incapacitating the men told to watch her only guaranteed them a few hours.

Firian's mind whirled with possible pathways, each one more difficult with Viv's presence. The forest, with its animals and snow-dropping trees, could keep an untrained eye from noticing their tracks. If there was a slaughterhouse or something nearby, that could effectively mask their scent, but he didn't know of one in the area. They were close to the ocean too, but much of it had frozen over. Boats weren't a viable option. But maybe ice was.

THREE HOURS LATER, Firian heard the ice crack. Sweat dripped down his back but he couldn't see the source of the noise. In his arms, Viv didn't stir. He knew how to survive if he fell through the frozen ocean surface, but he had no desire to relive that kind of experience. Time to get to shore.

Up to this point, he'd been treading as lightly as he could, first with the girl stepping carefully in his footprints, and then with the girl asleep in his arms. The shore was close now, close enough to risk an added measure of security. With each step, he kicked at the ice with his heel. Sloshing water and broken ice would hide their path, or at least make it more difficult to gauge. But the ice didn't crack again. He pounded harder as he stomped toward the shoreline.

The silence of the frozen water and jagged mountains and green-black sky had given him space to think. Suspended in that alien landscape, his mind finally felt clear again.

The deep night edged toward pre-dawn. He struck the ice again.

A moan, more than a crack, sounded beneath the ice like a subterranean beast. He thought, not for the first time, of the dark expanse of water below his feet. Would this whole night be full of monsters?

The moan became a creak keening from everywhere at once. He broke into a run.

Trees read as black lines against the black sky. Tiny lights like fireflies danced among them. Civilization, but remote. They'd be out of Ovkall, the settlement where the slaver had most of his operations, and maybe into Tilflagg, the neighboring town to the south.

At this point, it didn't matter. Sounds rose all around him. He'd started too soon. He needed to drop, spread out his weight, slide Viv across the ice. No, he was close enough to make it.

Panic threatened to claw up his chest. This was a bad idea. If the ice split and swallowed him, he could throw Viv before he fell and—

Hard ice gave way to pebbly ground beneath the snow. He kept running until he found grassy hillocks among the pine trees. Chest heaving, he leaned against a cold trunk and breathed in the fresh scent. It smelled like home.

Viv stirred. Behind him, the faint sounds of breaking ice echoed through the wilderness.

Bard would certainly be asleep, probably as deep asleep as this girl who didn't like him but had no choice but to trust him. Firian adjusted her weight, grateful that she kept his core warm enough to keep going despite the cold. His toes might not be so lucky.

"Bard!" he called into the Unreal.

Firian could go into Bard's dreams, but it was easier if Bard was actually awake. Dreams weren't reliable.

"Bard!"

"Mmm." The noise might not even have been a noise. More a feeling. Bard was waking up.

Firian recreated the harsh but picturesque landscape around him, giving it more light. "Bard, I need you to tell me who looked after Kader in Hinter. Was he in North Hinter, South Hinter...?"

Bard materialized, waving a hand sleepily to make Firian pause. A huge yawn broke over his face before he scratched the back of his head and focused, with effort, on Firian holding the figure of Viv in his arms.

"Fir," he slurred, shook his head. "Firian, what...? Are you okay?" He seemed to realize that Firian wouldn't contact him at this time of night without an emergency. Much of his sleepiness melted away into concern. "What's wrong? Who's that?"

"Viv. I told you about her."

"Right. What do you need?"

"The place where Kader stayed after the attack." He didn't need to explain which attack. They both knew too well about Master Belik's attempted coup two years ago.

Bard gazed around at the landscape. "It was South Hinter," he began. South Hinter was days away, practically a different country. It had more in common with their neighbors, the Endrians, than the North Hinterlanders did. Going there now would feel like retreat, since he still had business here with Gurthur, and Firian didn't retreat.

"The family was called Muller, I think," Bard continued. "They're just a normal family, not military, if I remember right. Cousin of Kader's nurse at the time, something like that. What do you need them for?"

"I need a safe place."

"For her?"

"Yeah." Even though he was in the Unreal and the real Viv couldn't hear him, he still lowered his voice. "I'm afraid her father wants to sell her off."

Bard blinked, forehead creasing with disgust.

Firian knew how the man worked, and now he had cut off his primary income, destroyed his investments, and scattered his company. Authorities knew Gurthur's name and were coming after him. He was cornered. All he had left was his exceptional daughter.

A non-warrior family couldn't take her now. The mad thought of bringing her back to the Academy crossed his mind. Absolutely not. What would he do afterward? Bring her up himself? He had a job to do that didn't include this little girl.

His big fur hat had fallen over her eyes as she slept. He needed to earn that childish trust.

To grow up with that man as a father...

Well, he knew a child couldn't choose their parents.

"Sell her off?" Bard repeated.

Firian realized he'd been silent for too long, thinking. "Yes. She's his only major asset now. I'm going to leave her with the authorities here and then find him before he can find her. We're too far away from South Hinter."

If Ortu Gurthur still had connections like the ones Firian already knew about, then Viv might not be safe with the authorities for long. It was time for him to cut the head off the snake, like he'd wanted to do from the beginning.

"Sounds like you've got a good plan." The sleepy tone had crept back into Bard's voice.

"I'll check in when it's done."

Firian rocked gently. Good thing Viv didn't seem to understand the words he'd exchanged with the man in the boathouse. A patrol cabin stood about an hour away. From there he'd set off to find the bastard and his buyer.

———

THOSE WEEKS of observation paid off. Process of elimination and consideration of the slavers' habits and methods had led here.

The door creaked quietly as it opened. Stone struck flint and a light flared to life. The two men coming through the doorway froze.

The buyer gasped.

"Who are you?" Gurthur demanded, fishing for a weapon.

Firian sat in the chair opposite the door, a dagger across his knees. He ran his finger casually across the blade. At last, he could finish the job. For Kiria, who needed this threat removed. For the slaves, who deserved to be free.

And for Viv.

A small smirk spread across Firian's face as he raised his head. "They call me the Ghost."

4

THE KEEPER AND THE PRINCESS

THE ROOM FELT HOT. Was it hot?

Behind these same shadowed and guarded double doors, Atty had waited for his coronation, but soon, this time, he wouldn't wait alone. Faint sounds of merrymaking built outside in the wide expanse of the Main. Why weren't there more lights in this little room? He wanted to see. The floor felt hard and the mirror leaning against one wall kept reflecting slivers of him that made his heart jump with anticipation before falling in disappointment. Not her.

Atty reached into his opulent white tunic and drew out the picture that hung there, the one that had kept him awake staring the night before. Twice he'd woken up, lain awake, lit the candle by his bed, looked at the picture, put out the candle again.

Now, he cracked open the bronze disk with a fingernail and looked one more time.

A young woman with dark red hair, almost black, gazed demurely just out of reach of his eyeline. She didn't smile, but her aspect looked peaceful. Maybe peaceful wasn't the right word. Her eyes flashed with serious thought, but she didn't seem distressed, rather... beautiful. There was another word, which

Kiria could have supplied, but beautiful was always the one that intruded. She was beautiful. Jori could tease him all he liked about how he'd never seen her in person and how the artist had glossed over the moles that made her look like a fairy tale villain. Atty wouldn't believe it.

She'd agreed to marry him. *Him.*

Yes, it was for an alliance, but Atty still couldn't believe his luck.

In the tiny portrait she wore stars in her hair, making her dark eyes bright. Like sparkling dust, they dotted just where her thick hair swept up into a partial braid. The artist had captured a loose strand that fell to her strong jawline.

His breath grew shorter as he cradled the necklace. Taking a deep, sugar-scented breath, he snapped the locket closed again and stuffed it into his shirt. Would she think he was cheesy for having her portrait made into this heirloom for himself? Would she like him at all? He wasn't as charismatic as Jori or as warm as Kiria. Despite being the oldest, he always lagged behind. At least, it felt like it.

Heat crept in again. The sound of guests beyond the darkened doors grew louder. Not long now. Dully, his heart thudded. He adjusted his shoulders, the white fur stole over one arm, his crown.

"I'm Atael Calthwaite." No, she knows that. "Hi, I'm Atty. So nice to meet you." He'd already tried so many variations of the greeting in his head.

Over the past week, he'd even done research on Haved Ganesha to find out as much as he could about the Charäkhni royal family, and her in particular. She was the second born of King Shear Ganesha, well respected and admired by her people, with a heart made of iron and still waters... The news was almost all vague like that, but he could feel himself falling, little by little, in love. The poem written for her on her fourteenth birthday—where he'd gotten the phrase "iron and still waters"—captured his imagination most. He'd had to find a young Charäkhni Amir-in-training for that particular piece of information.

A noise, quiet but unmistakably near, sounded in the adjoining office. Atty's pulse skittered. His hands felt big and unwieldy and his body absurd in this royal outfit.

It was Haved Ganesha. It had to be. What if he'd built her up too much in his mind? He'd be heartbroken. Or, what if she spent one day with him and was filled with bone-deep disappointment that her husband was only Atty and not someone better?

He swallowed, forcing breath in and out of his lungs. *Nothing you can do now.* The serenity of the inevitable came over him.

The side door opened.

Two people emerged, a Charäkhni soldier and a Kingdom guard, blocking his entire view.

"My Keeper," said the Kingdom soldier, bowing at the waist before nodding to the guards at the double doors as though they knew each other. He wore silver armor with a light blue swath of fabric across the shoulders, typical of palace guards, though Atty didn't know this one personally.

"Third Keeper Atael Calthwaite," echoed the Charäkhni soldier, pointed helmet intact so Atty couldn't see his expression clearly.

Atty fairly choked with impatience.

The soldier's thickly accented voice fell to a reverent hush. "This is Princess Haved Ganesha, son of King Shear Ganesha, of..."

The man might have said something else—a buzz in the air went on for a few beats longer—but that was when they moved out of the way.

Haved Ganesha herself stepped forward.

She looked even better than her picture. All in deep red, with a gem at her breast, she observed him, hands lightly folded. Coal lined her dark eyes. The skin of her cheeks and her tan throat looked smooth as water. Her lips were slightly drawn, the only sign that she might be feeling a fraction of the nerves he felt. She was almost as tall as he was so they met eye to eye. He could have looked and looked and looked. She was mystery and answer all at once.

He closed his mouth and blinked. All the words he had practiced were gone.

"I am pleased to meet you, Atael Calthwaite," she said, her voice low and accented. Her mouth curved in the barest hint of a smile.

"Atty," he responded, breathless. "That's what everyone calls me who knows me."

She was so composed, so elegant. He looked like some snow creature. Still, maybe it was his imagination, but he felt like there was something in her that responded to something in him, as though they'd known each other a long time or in another life.

"I'm glad you're here," he said, rallying.

"Thank you." She took another step forward.

"I was looking forward to meeting you."

"And I you."

"I asked everybody what they knew about you." He shrugged, keenly sensing her nearness as she stood beside him. She smelled like spices. It made him lightheaded, like laughing did when he couldn't take a breath.

"Lady Kiria and the Kepron, Jori?" she clarified.

He smiled to hear their names on Haved's lips. "They refused to tell me much of anything. But I wanted to know. I want to know you." His own boldness surprised him.

"And what do you want to know?" Her flirtatious tone left

him once again at a loss for words. His eyes dipped to the jewel on her chest, then back up. His cheeks flamed.

He struggled for a moment before her hand reached for his. "It will be all right," she said, even lower now.

He wanted to close the small gap between them and kiss her. Stomach twisting, he touched the side of her head with his fingertips, tracing the place where the painted stars had been. Her dark hair felt soft. Braver now, he did it again, this time starting at her cheekbone. She didn't flinch away from his touch. "You're not wearing stars in your hair."

"Not today," she replied mildly, with a small smile. "But I love them. You have strange stars here."

"Strange?" He heard her through a haze, as though he were slightly drunk.

"There are several stars new to me. Perhaps you can tell me about them?" Her brown eyes grew bright with eagerness.

"I can. I'll try." Atty loved looking at the stars, but he only knew the major constellations, not all the names. But he'd find out for her. They could sit outside on summer evenings, listening to the waves and watching the sky. The idea made him delirious with happiness. He caught his breath. "I'm glad it's you," he said, hoping she'd understand.

"I am glad that it's you, too," she whispered back.

Music, loud and sudden, burst forth from the Main. He'd almost forgotten. "Oh, um…" he started. "I wrote this song for you. For this. I know it's not very good, but I wasn't sure what you'd like…"

Haved pressed a swift kiss to his cheek, warm and sincere. A moment later, when he realized what he was doing again, his arm was around Haved's waist. The swell of her hip rested under his wrist. The music had changed from his simple melody to a traditional song of Brithnem.

"So far," said Haved, "I like you."

The double doors swung open and bright light poured in. Guests filled the space around the central dais, where several Amir waited, holding aloft a gauzy blue and white cloth. Soaring ceilings made the area feel open despite the crowd. Smells of sugar and champagne and perfume swirled around the two of them as they strode forward together into the Main.

He felt the metal of the little portrait warm against his chest. All these lights danced in Haved's hair and on the red gem and in her eyes. Not exactly stars, but close. Better. He watched her as they approached the steps to the platform. How did he get so lucky? Her beauty was through and through. She cheated a look back at him and it gave him a pleasant jolt in the pit of his stomach. It was time for an alliance.

5

———

SKUGGASTE

SUMMONING a spirit is harder than it sounds, especially when you have no idea how to do it.

Kader leaned over the boiling pot. The small branch of the *sachion* tree bobbed stubbornly at the top, refusing to break down at all. One of the palace cooks hovered nearby, kneading bread and casting looks at Kader and his friends, as if unsure whether she should step in and help. Hopefully she wouldn't. Taking a piece off a *sachion* tree, even for a royal Kepron, was prohibited.

"Stir it around," Metz suggested.

Kader already felt hot from the steam and the staring, but he took up a spoon and stirred. Technically, his two friends were his servants, but he hardly thought of them that way anymore. So, really, they should be the ones stirring the stick, but they knew he liked to be involved in the process. It felt as solid as ever as it knocked against the spoon. His hand grew hotter next to the boiling water.

"Did your mother tell you how long this part took?" Kader asked, looking at his other friend, Hob. Hob's shock of white hair floated above him as if he were underwater. It gave him the appearance of always being surprised.

"No. I figured it would be like boiling a potato."

"How long does that take?"

"Whole potatoes or diced?" Metz interjected. A line was beginning to form on his freckled forehead where the widow's peak stretched down. It was his researching look.

Kader frowned. They were getting off track. "Does it matter?"

"It does. One only takes about ten minutes but the other takes much longer."

Kader gestured at the pot with his spoon. "*This* much longer?"

"He doesn't know anything," said Hob, flicking a look at the cook who had begun eyeing them with more intensity. "The important part is that you have the branch. At least, I think that's what I heard. And my mother always said her grandmother had spices around the house. Those have to be part of it."

Kader turned to Metz. "You already have those, right?"

Metz rummaged through his pockets and drew out four small parcels neatly tied with string.

"Why didn't you take more?" asked Hob, elbowing him.

Metz elbowed him back, giving himself space. "I figured we shouldn't waste any. None of the sources I read talked about saddlebags of spices. That would be important to mention, don't you think?"

Kader sighed. "It's fine." Pain spasmed up his shoulder from the repetitive motion. He set the spoon aside. "This is taking ages."

Metz seemed to sense his meaning and began stirring for him.

Kader stretched his shoulders. The embroidered gray tunic felt tight across his chest. He was probably growing out of it again. Metz's uncle was a tailor and would insist it was no trouble, but Kader's rapidly growing body felt troublesome. Whenever he thought he'd peaked, his clothes wouldn't fit right anymore.

"I don't know," said Hob. "If you aren't patient, my mum used to say, the stars will come out without you."

Metz rolled his eyes. "We just need a little more time and then we'll try it. What do you think?"

"I think so," Kader agreed.

A thoughtful look crossed Hob's pale face. "I just... I just realized that my great-gran might have had those spices for keeping *skuggaste* away, not for summoning them."

Skuggaste. Spirits.

Metz looked at Kader. "They might be tied to the land—to Hinter. I've thought of that too."

"So have I," Kader shot back, more harshly than he meant. South Hinter was where he'd first heard of *skuggaste*. Everyone there seemed to believe in them, but his Amiran tutors hadn't mentioned them more than once, and even then it was only to give flavor to the mountainous land to the north. "*And they believe in mountain ghosts and spirits. Isn't that interesting?*" A fact isolated from reality.

But, years ago, when he was eleven, Kader had crouched there in hiding for several weeks, seeing murderous Tanyu in every shadow, even as he tried to mourn his family. Stories took his mind off the compulsive loneliness, the sense of being untethered and floating through black space. A Hinterlander family had taken him in, along with the guard and nurse who had escaped with him. It was an unseasonably cold autumn that year and frost crawled on the edges of the leaves and windowsills even as summer was coming to a close. Cupping a hot mug in his hands—tasted first by the guard to make sure it wasn't poisoned—he had listened to the Hinterlanders' stories. They told of heroes and monsters and villains, but Kader's favorites were about the spirits. Were they really the dead? Could they speak? Were they dangerous? Could anyone come back as a ghost?

He gazed down at the bubbling pot as Metz fished out the stubborn stick with tongs. It dripped on the counter.

"Put it there," Kader said, pointing. "Is there a way the spices are supposed to go?"

Hob gave an apologetic shrug.

"She's going to tell us off for not being more respectful," Metz whispered, watching the cook leave to another room. "I said that we should call him 'My Kepron' in public," he added to Hob.

"It doesn't matter," said Kader. "At least you don't call me Kade out here. When I'm Keeper, I'll change it so you don't have to be so formal around me." He prodded the stick with a finger. It was hot and damp, but little else had changed. "We've just got to work with this, I guess."

"Should we turn out the lights?" Metz asked smartly.

"Spices first," said Hob, untying the little parcels and pouring out the contents in rings around the *sachion* branch.

The result looked like a mess. If Kader were a spirit, he wouldn't come running just to see that. But he wasn't a spirit. They were different. They had to be handled carefully.

Metz had positioned himself by the lanterns flanking the door that led upstairs to the main level. He took the metal snuffer off its hook. "Good?"

"Good," replied Hob. "Ready?" There was a slight squeak to his voice that suggested he wasn't ready at all but wouldn't show it.

Kader nodded, a now familiar twist coiling in his belly. "Ready."

The lights went out, one after another. Kader heard his own breath, slightly labored, in the blackness. Only a rim of gold seeped in under the door to the adjoining room. Two guards waited just upstairs, another in the room next door. Kader had requested that they not be here for the experiment. He could never completely dismiss them, not after that day when he was eleven.

The tight feeling spread over his neck and down his spine. What would he see? Despite Hob having more knowledge than Kader did about Hinterlander folklore, he couldn't say much for certain about the *skuggaste,* only offer alternate stories. Most of those stories said the spirits were dangerous, though whether they were malicious or mercurial, no one knew for sure. No one even knew for sure whether the spirits were the essence of deceased people or something else entirely. Kader's heart beat erratically as he gazed out at the blank room. He hoped one of those was true.

Motes of light from the extinguished lanterns floated before his vision.

Was that something?

His blood chilled. He groped a numb hand through the wash of dark and found Hob's arm. "Do you see something?" he breathed.

The afterimage of light still hadn't faded, and now it seemed to be spreading, like a heavy blue cloud arranged in a pillar. A man-sized pillar. It couldn't be more than five strides away. He squinted into the place where a face should be but there was only blankness. The closer he looked, the less he saw. The whole figure faded when he stared.

Maybe Hob hadn't heard him. Maybe he was enthralled. Wasn't there something about—

Crash!

Kader jumped, tension arcing from his heel to his skull. The noise echoed through the empty kitchen, swiftly followed by the sound of Metz and Hob fighting to light the lanterns again. The door behind them opened. A guard stepped in.

Stabbing pain seized Kader, making him speechless, though curses rippled through his mind. His muscles contracted in that way they did when it felt like his own body attacking him, ripping him apart from the inside. Gripping the counter for support, he gasped in a breath of air. *Not again, not now.* The room slid in and out of focus. Only the burning slash across his back and neck seemed to mean anything at all. Muffled foot-steps blended with the heartbeat churning in his ears. He tried to stay upright, but only for a moment. He had to lie down. Had to stay still, with no pressure on his spine. Had to curl his knees up and rest his head on something soft.

The room was light. Hob bent to pick up the pot he'd knocked off the counter, his entire body chalk-white as he looked at Kader. Just a pot. The image was gone. Maybe it hadn't been there at all. *I had to be so damned afraid, didn't I?*

He lay on the hard floor, curled on his side. *Deep breaths.* Breathing wasn't automatic anymore, required all his mind but he couldn't spare a thought away from the spasm in his back. His arms shook with strain. Hot water soaked through his shirt, pooling under him. The boiling pot had water in it.

Figures stood above him, saying something. He looked away, closing his fingers into fists to stop the trembling. No position helped when the pain was like this. Normally a persistent ache, it rose to a roar more and more often.

Ever since he was eleven.

"WELL, THAT WAS ATTEMPT NUMBER FOUR." Metz's voice, a little gravelly from tiredness, came from somewhere to the left. He was probably curled up in the divan like a cat, cradling a brown leather book. That, at least, was his natural position when at rest. Kader suspected that Metz secretly liked the respite his painful episodes offered the others. Not that he liked to see Kader in pain, but it gave the opportunity for his friends to do things most servants in the palace never had time to do.

Kader pressed his head back into the soft pillow, trying not to move. The strain of keeping perfectly still made him ache. On the ceiling there was cloudily painted plaster, along with a small red mark which he remembered accidentally sending up there in a painting incident when he was seven or eight. He'd apologized to his nurse, but she never seemed to forgive him for it.

"Did you get the *sachion* branch, at least?" he asked.

"No," said Hob. His voice was slightly farther away, closer to the foot of the four-poster bed. "I forgot to grab it. By the time I could check, everything had been cleaned up."

Kader sighed. Stealing that branch from one of the potted trees in the great hallway had been borderline sacrilege. To do it again could start an incident with their allies in Enderin.

"But at least we saw something that time, right? You both saw something?"

"Sure," Hob agreed, but Metz only hummed dubiously. "I saw something," Hob insisted.

"I'm not going to count it unless I'm sure," Metz countered.

"I don't know that we'll be *sure*," said Hob. "Sometimes *skug-gaste* appear like glimmers on water."

"Glimmers on water?" Kader repeated, incredulously. "Before, you said they appeared in the shape of people. Like a mountain ghost."

"They can appear how they like." Hob's tone was defensive. "That's how they trick people."

An agitated rustling revealed that Kader had been right

about Metz being curled on the divan. "A glimmer on water could be a trick of the light, like when you stare into a flame before putting it out."

"What did you see, Hob?" Kader asked, slowly drawing up his knees and planting his feet flat against the covers.

"A sort of hazy light."

Metz snorted, but Kader's blood jumped with hopefulness. "That's what I saw too. About as tall as a person?"

"Maybe."

This was as close as they'd come to encountering a real *skuggaste*. A small smile curved Kader's mouth as he stared upward.

"Do you really think they're tricksters, Hob?" he asked. "Like sprites or something instead of people?"

A silence.

"If you're shrugging, I can't see you."

"Oh right. I don't know."

"You don't even know if they're glimmers," Metz said sulkily. "But if you two saw the same thing, then maybe they actually do exist. I've been writing down what we find. Imagine if it really worked! I would like to see that."

"And I want to finally tell my great gran I saw one."

Kader remained quiet.

"Kade?"

"I just want to see if we can do it." That wasn't strictly true. A tiny hope bubbled inside him that it wouldn't be just any spirit they summoned, but a couple of them in particular.

That is, if his body didn't give out first. Secretly, he feared that one of his episodes would be permanent, although doctors assured him that wouldn't happen. Most of the Kingdom didn't know about these bouts of pain that kept him cooped in his room for days, mysteriously absent from lessons with his Amiran tutor. The palace knew, of course, but he kept the truth as private as he could.

His father Cúron had been a strong Keeper his entire life, well respected by the people. Kader needed to be the same.

Friendly encouragement from Kiria, one of the current Keepers, to answer any questions he had about leadership or his father just made him sour. He should have had the chance to see his father lead firsthand. Now an Amir, Chetana, ruled in Kader's stead until he came of age next year.

Then he would have to sit on a throne all day, discussing policy and handing down judgments. It wasn't actually the politics he feared. He had a knack for that—probably in his blood. No, it was the visibility as he sat there. Many days, it wouldn't be a problem. A low hum of discomfort at the base of his spine and in his neck. Normal. That was what was left after his daily mix of teas and herbs. It was the other days that set his stomach crawling with dread. Maybe it would take a while, but eventually he'd go off like a bolt of lightning building invisibly in the clouds. His vision would blur and his back would spasm and it would be all he could do not to hit his head as he crumpled off the throne.

Some leader.

He flexed his toes into the silken covers.

"Metz, what do you think we should do next? The same thing?" he asked. Metz wasn't from Hinter, but he had better ideas for implementing Hob's theories.

"It wasn't very strong, if I couldn't see it."

"Isn't there a *sachion* tree in the little reception room?" Hob asked.

Kader racked his memory. Besides the Main, people most often met in the adjacent dining area with its long table. But there was another room, largely unused, on the far end of the palace, in the Third Keeper's wing.

"I think so."

"Why couldn't we use that?"

Kader's eyebrows shot up. Why hadn't he thought of that before? He hadn't needed to desecrate a branch after all. "Yeah! Let's try it."

"Two days?" asked Metz. They were used to Kader's episodes by now.

Kader shifted his body on the bed. Two days should do it. "Yes."

"I'll get rid of the guards," said Hob.

"We can't get rid of the guards," Kader put in at the same time Metz laughed.

"You sound like you're going to kill them," he said.

"I could if I wanted to," Hob replied, defensive.

"Oh please. Would you bore them to death?"

"My dad works at a smithy, remember. He makes swords."

"Which aren't here."

"I could ask him."

"And then you'd fight trained guards?"

"How would you do it, then, *Metzli*?"

"Poison. Nobody would know."

"How would you get them close enough to smell your breath?"

"Ha ha. I have some bugs in my collection that would—"

Kader lay still as they argued. A muscle just below his shoulder blade was slowly twisting, twisting, like a garrote.

Hob was the first to notice. "Kade? Are you all right?"

Kader's eyes closed tight shut. "Run a hot bath," he gritted. A quiet shuffle and he could tell they had run to do as he asked.

He'd survived this before. In two days he'd be back to normal and they'd try summoning the spirit again. At least he had something to look forward to, and friends willing to try this mad experiment to see his parents one last time.

THE MEETING ROOM lay dark in the twilight. It had only one window that looked out at a few trees that clustered like a mini forest against the wall surrounding the palace grounds. Some of the shivering leaves twinkled with faint light reflected from the rooms still lit on that side of the castle.

Inside the room, a few cushioned chairs lined up against the walls in small groups as though they were whispering together. Lanterns ringed the walls just above head height. At Kader's command, Hob lit one.

Their activities here were only partially clandestine. Guards had followed them and now stood just outside the door, ready to rush in at the least sound of disturbance. The guards' edginess caused the three of them to practically walk on tiptoe in their effort to be quiet. Ghosts and guards had that effect.

Technically, it wasn't forbidden to raise a spirit. But, unofficially, it was frowned upon as a semi-pagan practice. If people really could come back and communicate to the living, though, why shouldn't one try it? If *skuggaste* were people. Hob didn't seem to think so. Based on his darting eyes and hollow breathing, they might have been freeing a giant flying lizard with a taste for human flesh. Metz coolly oversaw every aspect of the operation that Kader didn't direct himself.

They had spices, just as they had the other night, and a bucket of hot water set at the foot of the potted *sachion* tree.

Kader stretched and popped the bones in his back. As predicted, he felt back to normal.

"Is it late enough?" Metz quietly asked Hob, who shrugged.

"I think so."

Metz rolled his eyes. "You don't have any idea about these spirits, do you?"

"No one does!"

"They would if they existed," Metz muttered.

"No one's an *expert*," Hob amended.

Kader took up the first spice bag. "We've had four tries. This one has to work."

The sound of Kader's voice seemed to snap the other two out of their bickering and set them back to work.

"You said you saw something last time?" Metz whispered.

"Mmm." Kader didn't meet his eyes, focused instead on the spice ring he was creating around the shadowy tree.

"A man-sized shape," Metz provided, following close behind with the second spice.

Kader's chest tightened for some reason. It felt like embarrassment. "Yes," he confirmed, shaking off the feeling. The air smelled stale and dusty. He rolled his shoulders. No matter what appeared—and hopefully something did—he wouldn't seize up or flinch. It could be a creature with the body of a snake and the head of a bear and he'd just look it coolly in the face.

Hob's chest rose and fell quickly. Nerves.

"I don't think bringing water to a branch is the same thing as bringing a branch to the water," Metz declared, tapping the little bucket with the toe of his shoe.

"But spirits appear in the forests. There aren't any buckets there," said Kader. "Just water."

Hob nodded.

Metz shrugged assent. "Maybe you're right. Kade, you should do it, then."

Though the room smelled musty, the tree itself, when Kader got closer, had a sharp healthy smell. It energized him. "Okay," he said, picking up the bucket.

Hob bit his lip. "Here we go."

"Try number five," Metz added, like a performer waving on the main act.

The water sloshed as Kader lifted it to a downward jutting

branch. Cradling the bucket in both hands, he held it up until the branch soaked down into the water. Little rings emanated from where the branch broke the water's skin.

"*Skuggaste*," Hob whispered, as though calling them out of a hiding place.

Metz looked on impassively, clinically, his freckles dark in the dim light. Maybe he was thinking of a better way to hold the bucket. The furrow of his eyebrow, though, betrayed a twinge of interest. Despite his arguments with Hob, Metz wanted the *skuggaste* to be real almost as much as Kader did.

A minute passed.

There was a soft shuffling noise of feet. Kader turned his head. Just the guards outside the room. The rustling of leaves and Hob's short breaths. The small lap of water. Kader was careful not to smudge the circle of spices with his boots. The result was a slightly uncomfortable position that grew more uncomfortable as time passed and he still held the bucket up to the tree, trying not to move.

Please. Father, mother... His pleading sounded desperate and pathetic, even in his own head. They wouldn't appear. And he wasn't a child calling for them anymore. Years had passed since their sudden deaths. He was a young man now, nearly old enough to ascend to the throne himself. But did anyone truly outgrow their desire to know and impress their parents, or to say goodbye?

In his peripheral vision, something moved. It could have been small as a dust mote, but bright and swiftly moving. He looked sharply at the others. The looks of concentration on their faces confirmed that they thought they'd seen something too.

Kader's heart sped up. The water around the branch rippled. He slowly drew air in from his nose and loosened his back and shoulders.

A tinkling, like tiny, far-off bells grew in his mind until it became a real sound. Now he nodded at Metz and Hob, whose eyes had both grown round. They nodded back. Metz's fingers twitched as though desperate for a pen. No one spoke, afraid to break the spell.

In the lantern, the flame sputtered, but there was no wind. Now Kader had to fight to keep his breathing even. This was something. This was *something*! He scanned the room, taking care to move his head slowly.

The light in the lantern went out. Hob jumped. Metz reached out to steady him. At the same moment, a face, indistinct, appeared, glowing like a reflection in the window. The glint of eyes burned faintly. The suggestions of a mouth, straight nose, high cheekbones, all not quite in focus, were otherworldly. The gender of the creature was unclear. It didn't look like a person. Almost, but not quite. It was too large, too bright. The eyes were set too far apart. The skin could have been green or blue or white or black for all Kader could see.

A quiet splashing sound brought him back to an awareness of the room where he stood with numb feet. He didn't look away from the thing at the window. If he did, he felt it would disappear like a forest creature into the dark.

They stared at each other, Kader's heart and breath stuttering.

"Who are you?" it asked in a voice like water or wind. Or maybe the question was "*what* are you?"

It was talking. It was talking to him. "I'm Kader Calthwaite," he breathed, not daring to blink.

The figure didn't respond, but only canted its head slightly and blinked.

It didn't disappear, not exactly. It lingered. Sometimes it seemed as though parts of it were in the room with them. Other times, it seemed outside, far away. But gradually, it wasn't there.

Like the deep darkness before dawn, it seeped away imperceptibly, until Kader found himself staring at nothing.

His arms were shaking. He let out a long breath and lowered the bucket.

Hob squeaked, a sort of crazy laugh. "Was that... you *talking* to it? What were those noises you were making?"

"What noises?" Kader asked.

"The whispery sounds."

Metz still stared at the window. "You all saw that?" he whispered.

"Yeah." Kader nodded. "What was it?"

"Fifth time's magic," Hob put in, breathless.

"I don't know." Metz raised his eyebrows as though stretching them. "I don't know what that was. Obviously, we have to repeat—"

"*Skuggaste,*" Hob interrupted. "It wasn't a person."

"No." Kader looked behind him but the room was so dark he could barely see anything. Was there a way that a person could have made that reflection and fooled them all? No. And there were the bells, and there was the alien regard of the thing, the hazy outline. All of it implied that this wasn't a trick. He set down the bucket. In his amazement, he'd shuffled some of the spices out of line. A glittering spray of red, black, and yellow spread inward toward the planter holding the tree. "And you both saw it," he confirmed again.

"Yeah," said Hob. "You doing all right?"

Kader paid attention to his body again. He felt stiff, and his arms shuddered from the strain of holding the bucket, but that was all. He reported this.

"We just saw a spirit, I think," Metz said, head tilted down as he obviously tried to sift through his thoughts. "And, Kade, were you talking to it?"

"It... You heard it, right? It asked who I was." Even as he said it, that didn't feel like the right translation. *Translation? It was speaking the common tongue, wasn't it?*

"What did you say?" Hob's round eyes looked crazed.

"My name." Kader's mind whirled. Could the others really not understand the creature?

"You introduced yourself to it?" Metz asked, barely containing his excitement now. "Did it tell you who it was?"

Kader frowned. "No. Stop joking around."

"We're not!" Hob insisted.

A new expression formed on Metz's face. "You don't think this means..."

"What?" Kader demanded.

"This isn't Original Language, is it?"

"No. Couldn't be." Kader hadn't heard of anybody in the last fifty years who'd had the divine gift of Original Language. But, Abilities did run more strongly in royal bloodlines, and he had just talked to the spirit when the others couldn't understand it... Was it possible? "You think?" he amended.

"That sounds like what this is."

"We couldn't understand it at all. We were frozen solid," Hob said.

"Maybe next time we can try to talk to it," Metz suggested.

Next time. In the wake of the supernatural apparition, a wild calm had settled over Kader. He felt full—full of thoughts, full of awe. Like smoke creeping in through slats in a floorboard, the idea came that this spirit was not his parents. Not Cúron or Varinna. It was something utterly different. He'd found more questions instead of answers. But, oddly, he wasn't disappointed.

It was like climbing up a hill to find a grave and finding not that, but many more hills on the horizon. More countries, even, with separate moons.

To be Kader Calthwaite, Kingdom heir in pain, was too

limiting a designation. Yes, he was the Kepron. Yes, his body rebelled against him. But his identity waited elsewhere, seemingly limitless. His veins felt filled with life and the earth filled with marvels.

6

———

FEROCITY

BELIK AND CHETANA'S STORY

"GET UP! You can't sleep the day away!"

Chetana's throat tightened with irritation and she rolled over toward Gerand's side of the bed. A layered thudding meant she'd accidentally pushed the books off the shelf. Her little collection barely fit in the space she'd made for them over the empty half of the cot. *Gerand's side.* She needed to stop thinking of it that way. Her sister was long gone.

The effort of turning pulsed the blood in her head and she stopped, squeezing her eyes shut and taking a steadying breath through her nose. It wasn't just the headache. It was the sense of wrongness, as though her long limbs had been stretched out of shape, or she had ingested poison. Everything hurt.

She eased herself into a sitting position, straightening her spine, and leveled a dark gaze at the speaker. In the doorframe stood a powerful woman with light skin and white dreadlocks. As usual, Maal's legs spread apart and the muscles in her arms flexed, ready for action. Chetana's muscles had hardened since coming here too, but she was a different kind of soldier. Maal had never understood that.

"Is the meal prepared?" Chetana asked in a voice clipped by annoyance.

"We finished hours ago. You have a new assignment."

Already? "I completed the last one less than a week ago."

"Are you arguing with me? In your place, you know I'd do it." Maal's eyes flicked toward the fallen books. Her thoughts were written on her face. *Your sister is a traitor. Are you?*

"We can't afford to shirk," Maal continued. "The mission is too important."

In this, Chetana had to agree. She bowed her head once, a tiny concession. Original Plan was the Khelê's only hope. The group had taken her in when no one else would, a dark-skinned Khelê girl in King's Heights, where uniformity was touted as purity and tradition. Aberrations like her were barely tolerated. Sometimes, they were violently opposed, just for their differences.

Jyföring, they called her. *Child of shame.* It was an old word, dating back to the beginning of the Khelê, when the Kingdom didn't understand they were God's gift, not his punishment. The ugly slur stirred fire in her heart any time she heard it. It reminded her of the plan—God's plan, the Original Plan for the Khelê to be united.

Something sour rose in the back of Chetana's throat. She swallowed it back down. What had to be done had to be done. The words rang repeated like a mantra among the women, and Chetana lived by them as much as anyone else. Maybe even more, since she had more to overcome. Gerand had made Chetana an outcast among outcasts, and she hated her for it.

"What is the mission?"

BELIK WAVED his fingers idly through the floating flames—thumb, 2, 3, 4, 5—back and forth. The fire rippled in response like orange smoke around his hand, dispersing before reforming into a loose ball. At a thought, it turned from orange to blue. The ghostly light washed his thick forearm sickly pale. The hairs left shadows.

The mission was simple. Not easy, but simple. Let her into his mind.

Frankly, he was glad for the assignment. The directive in these situations was almost always to deny a connection, steel one's mind against the possibility of a deadly *katah*. But the Head himself trusted Belik with this task. If he could bring down the group that had caused the Tanyu so much trouble the last six months, then... He smiled.

Then he would be the next in line.

It was a natural move from Strategy Master to Head of the Tanyuin Academy. This mission would prove him ready.

"Ah!" A piercing burn thrilled through his hand. He sucked in a sharp breath. The flames vanished.

Belik opened his eyes, coming out of the Unreal back into reality. Irritated, he looked down at a dark red spot blooming in the center of his palm.

Careless.

He closed his fingers over the burn. What a Learner's mistake! Heat spread to his neck. When she came, he couldn't allow a moment of abstraction. These women were Original Plan's best assassins. A moment of believing her reality and he'd be killed.

Maybe it wouldn't be so hard. This wasn't the first time someone had declared *katah* on him. The idiots had sent a young girl—just finished with her training, no doubt—who simpered and agreed with anything he said. Skin and bones, no trademark sensuality. When she came to his dreams and touched him, he felt nothing but revulsion.

It had been easy to kill her.

Belik flexed his hand over the wound. In the Unreal, he would erase it, make it just like before with the same callouses, nails picked back, scars over the middle knuckles of his right hand.

The shadows thickened in the stone house. Sias Jairon had paused most strategy assignments so Belik could focus on getting this done. Without his usual work, restlessness over-whelmed him. Maybe it was best to sleep, open his mind, and let this poor woman in.

SHE CAME THAT NIGHT.

Already, she looked completely different from the last one. The green dress she wore had a high neckline and paneled skirt, more like a warrior's outfit than a coquette's. Through the slats of the long skirt, he saw yellow shoes—flat and practical, but bright. With her short curly hair, she stood a little taller than he was. Tall, and strong too. Her exposed arms and what he could see of her calves were well muscled. High cheekbones made her almost regal. An intricate metal septum ring completed the picture of war-hardened royalty.

At first, she regarded him as one would look at a coming storm, wary but interested, loving the sound of thunder but also prepared to weather its advances. The sheen of a smile covered her face, though it didn't show on her full lips.

She sized him up, eyes raking down his body, her dark brown eyes only a little darker than her skin. She had a severity he recognized somehow.

"Master Belik," she said. Her low voice would have been soothing, if not for the military edge.

One side of his mouth lifted in a dark smile. "You know my name."

"I know a lot of things."

The steps they took forward felt like choreography, or the careful steps of predator and prey. At least he liked this prey better than the last. For all her initial secrecy, she didn't pretend this was something other than the declaration of *katah*. So how did she plan to make him want her, need her? He remained fully aware of what was Real and Unreal, even though he dreamed of a building very like his own house. Years of experience had taught him to plant clues, wrong details, so his subconscious wouldn't get confused.

"I should know your name," he said.

"Chetana," she replied. One name. Either she wanted to keep the family name a secret or she was Khelê. He suspected the latter. One Khelê knew another. Or half-breed, as he was.

She turned her head, distracted. "What's that?" she asked casually.

He followed her gaze. It was the blue pot he had placed in his house to remind himself that he was in the Unreal. "It's for cooking oil."

She tipped her lip at his answer. Maybe she could tell he was lying. "What's this?" she said, stepping within inches of him. He didn't retreat, even as their bodies almost touched. She raised one hand and smoothed her thumb over his forehead near the hairline. Her skin smelled like sandalwood.

"A mole," he replied flatly. This inane question-and-answer session was a typical gambit. He'd done the same thing—get the enemy to answer innocent questions so they would answer the serious ones too, sometimes without realizing the shift. His turn. "Are you Khelê?"

She half smiled, her top lip curling around the septum ring. This close, her eyes looked tired. "Yes."

"From Brithnem?" A high concentration of Khelê lived in the capital.

When she shook her head, a few curly hairs brushed his face. "No."

He was known for his patience, but he wanted to find a crack in Chetana's armor. Why wait for the inevitable? "How many times have you declared *katah*?"

She didn't flinch. Even her large dark eyes, a hand-breadth from his own, showed no surprise. "I have killed many men." She said it clearly, slowly, without remorse. So young to have that answer. Twenty-one, at most.

A red twisting in his core responded to her words. His heart thumped once, twice, six times before he calmed it down.

Much more impressive than the last one.

DID BELIK KNOW GERAND? There had been something like recognition in his eyes when he first saw Chetana. The sisters didn't look similar, but small traits and habits still passed from family to family. Hopefully his look was more than merely recognizing her exhaustion.

She had done this before—link minds with an enemy only to tear herself away and leave the target as nothing but a shell, half their own life ripped away in the process—but tonight had disconcerted her.

In her room, the rock walls smelled musty. It must have rained in the night. There was no way of knowing for sure. Besides strategically placed ventilation holes, there were no openings to the outside world. Chetana rarely saw the sky anymore. She needed air.

Steadying herself on the mattress, she stood on trembling legs. She'd never tried visiting the Unreal so soon after a completed *katah* before. If the women continued to use her this often as a weapon, surely she would flare out and fall into ashes. The comfort of her bed drew her in, but she needed strength more. Her stomach felt hollowed out. She forced herself toward the door. For as long as she was able, she would press on for the cause.

The corridor stared back to her in darkness. She felt her way forward by memory to the food stores. The watery smell intensified here, but, joining it, was the smell of toasted bread. She knitted her brows and turned the final corner.

A knot of sister-members sat close together at the small round table. In its center was a paper with a map and notations. Everyone looked up when Chetana entered.

Dilly, who did most of the cooking, leapt off Pandora's lap. "Chetana!" she cried, as surprised to see her as Chetana was to see Dilly awake at this time of the night, before dawn. "You must need some food."

"I do." She stood with her back to the wall so her posture didn't display her weakness.

With his experience, Master Belik must have sensed her weakness. He certainly seemed sure of himself around an assassin.

"I'll get you toast, eh?"

"Thank you."

The others didn't appear so apt to please Chetana, but acted as though she had interrupted something important. Pandora rubbed the place where her knee would have been had she been born with an entire right leg. Khelê tattoos webbed the skin there.

Chetana didn't ask what they were doing, just as they never asked what she was doing. Sometimes they told each other, but targets in King's Heights and targets of the mind were different. They existed in separate worlds.

Despite their vast differences, all members lived alike in their pursuit. It was a family—*her* family—for lack of any better.

Once she'd gathered enough breath, she crossed the room to heat water for tea. The smell of buttery char rose near Dilly's bustling form, but the other women remained stubbornly silent.

She knew people like Maal and Pandora did not hide their bitterness that those with the ability to perform *katah* were the best chance they had at taking down the infamous Tanyuin Academy. Since its location was secret, Original Plan couldn't send in actual warriors.

Honestly, Chetana was glad. Tanyu were reputed to be the best fighters in the world. No one could fault the heart or drive in these women, but against trained warriors, against Tanyu, they'd fall.

No, better to make smaller attacks against King's Heights, where all of them had experienced persecution. Chetana and the others would rot the Tanyu from the inside and, one glorious day, Original Plan's dream would come true. The Tanyu would fall and the Khelê would be free from the blight of the Split, when the Khelê fractured into Amir and Tanyu: Amir for wisdom and Tanyu for defense. Soon afterward, the Tanyu, glutted by greed, forsook their sacred calling and became an army of traitors. Old books told the story.

Once the Tanyu were eradicated, the Khelê could heal. It would take years, but the strength of a cause wasn't determined by how quickly it could be accomplished. Often the greatest changes grew slowly, like the cavern room where she stood, eroded by time and ancient workmen's tools.

Dilly passed her a plain slice of toasted bread. The first delicious bite confirmed how famished she'd become after her last *katah*. To face Master Belik again would require strength and a sharp mind. "Thank you," she said again, and poured tea before returning to her room alone.

By the time she reached the bottom of the teacup, she felt revived. The image of Master Belik returned to her, with his keen gaze and hard features and insufferable pride, as though she were an insect to be examined before eradication. He had been ready to see her, but not excited, as some men were. The last thing she felt like doing around him was to flirt, but that always had to be her first tactic.

She set down her cup, pushing away her trepidation and distaste.

It was a shame the Tanyu were so popular. Their evil had a gloss and glamour that could seduce even a member of Original Plan, if they received an invitation to be tested for the Academy.

Chetana had received a letter. She'd burned it in the fireplace across from her now. A whole night spent stoking the flames, adding fuel, strengthening the fire again, never letting it get low. The letter was a curse, and she wanted it gone beyond anyone's ability to find or sense it. Even her own. The room had grown so hot that night. Beads of sweat had trickled down the shaved sides of her head.

When fuel had run out, she'd ripped off her wooden cuff and thrown it in. Then a book. Then a pair of shoes her sister had left behind.

Gerand. Who had abandoned her to join the enemy.

Chetana stood suddenly, forcing herself out of her reverie. With so much at stake, there was no time for these reflections. She was an assassin, and a good one. Master Belik, killer of two members of Original Plan already, was the most advanced target she'd been assigned yet—the Strategy Master for the Tanyuin Academy—but she could destroy him.

A REPLICA OF CHETANA—IF that was her real name—stood like a statue in the Unreal. It wore the same outfit, down to the septum ring in her nose.

"That's what she looks like," Belik said abruptly, interrupting his own inspection of the figure. No need to dwell on someone who would be gone soon.

Across from where Belik conjured the vision, Sias Jairon rubbed his chin thoughtfully. Faint light emanating from the figure of Chetana glinted dully off his crown—nothing but an iron circle with an open square in front. One day, that crown would pass from Sias to Belik.

They both stood in black space. It might be more entertaining to stretch the imagination, but it was more pragmatic not to create a background apart from the blackness. That way, all focus could be on Chetana.

Standard procedure demanded that Belik disclose any attempted *katah* against him so everyone would be able to recognize the threat for who they were. Well, at least Sias could recognize them. He was the only one who insisted on knowing. For someone so introverted, the Tanyuin Head liked to know about every person associated with the Academy, even tangentially.

"I know her." Sias drew out the words, as though trying to place her. Then his gaze cut to Belik. "Chetana. She's Gerand's sister."

Belik's brow twitched. Gerand was a girl who came to the Academy soon after he'd arrived. They hadn't talked much, but he admired her seriousness and focus. She didn't cajole like other students. Instead, she had the attitude of someone hardened in battle or betrayal. He liked her.

Gerand, however, had light, even grayish, skin. He'd never seen her wear her long hair down. Chetana had rich, dark skin, and that was only the beginning of a list of differences between the two women. Unless Belik counted something in their expression, their features didn't match. Chetana's eyes, nose, and lips were all larger and the effect more beautiful. Her hair was curly and worn so short he could see the tattoo etched into the side of her head. She was taller, her face more oval, her square-cut jaw more appealing. Gerand studied the art of *katah* but Chetana had more natural assets.

The family connection shouldn't have surprised him as much as it did. Khelê never did look the same.

Belik resettled his glasses on his nose. "How do you know her?"

"She rejected the offer to be Tested."

Now, that was interesting. She preferred to stay with Original Plan than to join the Tanyuin Academy. Something dark stirred in his belly at the idea. To refuse such a privilege was as close to sacrilege as he could imagine.

Gerand's sister. Belik could use the connection to his advantage. Tonight, he'd go knowing something about her and give up nothing about himself. Without a foothold, she would fall harder into his trap.

He looked again at the image in the darkness. The unseeing eyes stared straight ahead with that calm intensity that wanted to draw him in. What could she do in the Unreal? Suddenly, he looked forward to the night.

CHETANA SCHOOLED her breathing before she met Belik again. She couldn't start out angry, but that's what she was. Gerand had been on her mind all day, as well as the women Belik had already killed like so many sparrows.

Master Belik had immediately struck her as someone who didn't mind anger. The most interest he'd shown in her during their first encounter was the moment she'd let some of her bitterness and exhaustion show. *I've killed many men.* His eyes had lit up in that greedy way she knew well.

Anger made her careless. It didn't matter if he liked it. Perhaps it was the vulnerability behind emotion that he liked so much, which gave him a way under her skin. She wouldn't give him one this time. Instead, she would approach him calmly and confidently, and she would learn about him, and she would ingratiate herself into his life piece by piece before she tore it away.

The thought still lingered in her mind like a talisman when he appeared, quick as breath. His sharp eyes met her own with a shrewdness that belied his youth.

A muscle in her neck tightened. It was the middle of the night. Was he not asleep? Most dreamers took a while to notice her.

The Unreal intersected with dreams so she could access his if she tried. It was a typical gambit. Go to the subject when their defenses were down. Most women used physical closeness then. It was the easiest and fastest way to intertwine their two minds, meld them into one so that the target became co-dependent. That had been the other girls' strategy with Belik, and they'd only lasted a couple weeks.

"You're here already?" she asked smoothly.

"A Tanyu is always ready for an attack." The slight gravel in his voice wasn't from sleep. That tone had been there yesterday. Everything about Belik was rough, from his voice to his skin to the solid muscles of his broad frame. Chetana forced herself to linger on them. Let him think she wanted him. Then, when she didn't give him what he asked, maybe they could get somewhere. She wouldn't make the same mistakes as the others, who all deserved better than death at the hands of this man.

"This isn't an attack," she replied, dropping her eyes and drawing another breath. Anger rose up in her chest like fire, and

Belik hadn't even done anything new to spark her ire. "I'm just here to talk."

Belik gave a barely constrained sigh. Had he hoped it would be an attack?

"Is it cold where you are?" she asked, nodding to his long-sleeved black shirt and pants.

"I don't prefer to talk."

A shoot of ice rinsed down Chetana's spine. So it was like that? She held her ground, though her instincts warred, loudly insisting that she move farther away from him, or else move closer. The moment called for something definitive.

Belik's gaze lifted away from her to the vague gray expanse above them. Gentle snow began to fall, chilly on her skin. Huge flakes stuck in her hair and on her clothes. When she looked down again, they stood together in a forest like the one a couple hours away from King's Heights. The woods looked tidy somehow—the trees too uniform and the ground a sheet of dulling green. It was dusk. Beside them rested a squat cabin with an overhanging roof, beneath which were two chairs.

Chetana looked at Belik suspiciously. They both knew why they were here. Only one would survive this months-long dance, and Belik's attitude, his every motion, said he wasn't sentimental. He didn't plan to lose.

"Beautiful," Chetana admitted, sitting in one of the chairs so she could look out. The chairs were almost large enough for two people. That fact was clearly a tacit invitation for her to use as she saw fit. She saw fit not to use it at all. The thought of him beside her brought tension to her shoulders. Resting on her hip, she draped herself sideways to look at the other chair. That way, she'd take up all the space and still focus entirely on him.

Belik sat. For a while, she studied his profile as he looked out at the falling snow. His jaw was rigid, as though he tasted some-thing bitter. Light fell on his face and the backs of his hands as he rested them on the chair. His short-cropped brown hair stuck flat against the back of his neck and straight out above the temple of his glasses. There had to be something about him that she could cling onto until this was done—a shred of humanity or attractiveness...

Right now, snow was falling, and he'd made that. It was the best she could do.

"I love looking out at snow like this," she said low in her throat. "I used to sit on a particular rock as a child where we could observe all weather undisturbed. Snow was my favorite."

Get your voice in his head. Get him to talk about his childhood. Make him think you fawn over him. Validate the self-congratulatory thoughts he has about himself.

Chetana had never written them down, but she'd learned maxims from this kind of work that could speed the process of a *katah*.

"Although, sometimes we were content to watch birds on a cloudy day as well." Memories welled up as she said it. Her big sister's arm around her as they watched for new species or tracked their paths across the sky.

Vulnerability from one coaxes it from both parties.

"It did not have to be an interesting day like this for us to sit together away from everything and appreciate the beauty of the world." She realized she kept saying *we*. Would Belik put the pieces together? Well, he would eventually, if she lived long enough. She stiffened despite her reclined position in the chair.

Belik's face didn't betray any emotion or recognition. It was almost as if he couldn't hear her.

"Did you have a place like that?" she asked.

He ignored the question, gesturing instead to the landscape with an impatient movement. "Can you add to it?" He said it as though she should already have done something, anticipated him.

Swallowing down her irritation, she sat up and switched her attention outward. Belik liked prowess. Several pieces of evidence corroborated it so far.

"I can add to the landscape if I wish," she replied.

Silence followed. She sat stubbornly still.

Finally, he turned to her. His face had barely changed, but there was an unmistakable narrowing of his eyes. "You said you could change something."

"You didn't make a request."

Belik merely flicked his hand toward the snow.

Chetana's blood heated. He didn't take her flirtatious bait. Instead, he treated her like some misbehaving child. She bit her tongue to stop herself from lashing out. Doing so now would place herself in undue danger. This man was a trained Tanyu and, hateful as they were, that meant that he began with the upper hand in the Unreal. Her mission was to dismantle that advantage, and that took time.

She rubbed her lips together to hide their scornful lift. After one moment to appreciate the loveliness of the snowfall, she changed it to rain. It splashed softly just outside the awning. Cool mist sprayed her bare ankles. The effect soothed her.

It was a poor idea to let down her guard and focus only on the background of the Unreal. For her, it took mental energy to keep the illusion going. But he looked at her, and the exercise gave her a reason to look away from him. Those were good moves in this game, both ways.

The trees took on more textured bark. Clouds floated overhead. Flowers budded among the grass. The forest didn't look perfectly real, but it tasted more like reality.

They sat in silence the rest of the night. She didn't like small talk either.

CHETANA REMAINED in Belik's mind, buzzing there like a painless Sentry. She was with him when he ate, when he talked to other Masters, when he jogged, when he slept. Though he wasn't a *katah* Master himself—more suited to strategy—he could mull on a problem long after many gave up on it. So he kept up his guard, deflecting all of her questions, and there were many of them.

After the first few meetings, they didn't talk much, but she would confide in him and then ask about him. What did he fear? Who did he love? What was he proud of?

He answered nothing.

She offered nothing else.

The first woman who had declared *katah* on him had come in sheer dresses. He hadn't needed to imagine what was beneath. Though he would physically respond, mentally she had no hold on him. Lust was pleasurable but not distracting.

Chetana was different. She never kissed or touched him. Maybe that was why he thought about her more insistently. She aggravated him, always holding back her ability in the Unreal. Clearly, she had Talent, but he wanted to see the full scope of what she could do. Instead, she asked about his family, his work, his home. It would be easier if she didn't play coy but gave him something he wanted. This feeling that she and her Talent were always just out of reach niggled at his mind, despite the constant sense of her presence.

Three weeks had passed since their first meeting. Belik slipped into a light sleep, searching for Chetana. Their time would soon run out, but until then, he could uncover secrets about Original Plan, learn more about Talent users outside the Academy, and gain information about Gerand, who was a rising star among the Tanyu, though relatively unpopular. Always a good idea to gather intelligence on allies and enemies just in case.

Ribbons of bright, translucent color flowed like streams of water through the blackness of his dream, intertwining and flying apart. Red and green and blue and gold. Watching the patterns snake through the air mesmerized him into rest, even when his mind roiled with problems he had to solve for Sias. He floated with the streams, suspended among them. The air smelled rich and sweet.

Constant vigilance had been a feature of Belik's life for as long as he could remember, but here, he was nothing, a mote in eternity.

"What is this place?"

Belik turned, slow and thick as water, to face Chetana, who floated too. All this time and she hadn't shown him she could do that. His defenses snapped back up, natural as breathing.

"Nothing."

The abstract dreamscape dissolved. In its place rose a series of red and gold platforms, arranged at intervals with walls strewn at random like a maze. The levels rose on tiny spindles so high that their bases disappeared into mist. Some platforms could barely accommodate two feet. Others stretched as large as a manor house. Above them, the sky glowed dark blue and mauve.

Belik and Chetana stood in a space the length of two men, with a wall along one side and a stomach-turning drop on the other three. If his ingenuity impressed her, she didn't show it. Maybe this alien landscape would jar her into revealing more of her skills. There was plenty to play with here.

Her dark eyes looked a little sunken today. Seeing her every night and sensing her every day gave him an acute awareness of her that he wasn't sure he liked. *She* was the maze, yet she rarely revealed the intelligence so clearly etched into her every line.

"I talked to your sister today," he said. Gerand had lingered at the edges of many of their brief conversations, but had never taken the forefront. Today, Belik was tired of waiting. Let this topic jar her out of whatever inane pattern of questioning she'd try next.

Chetana's full lips tightened. "What did you talk about?"

"Don't you want to know how she is? You never talk to her. What if I'm lying and she isn't even here at the Academy? She just wanted to leave you." The words fell out of him in a torrent.

Chetana lowered her head like an animal about to strike, eyes flashing hatred. It was a look beneath the careful mask she always put on. Her chest rose and fell more quickly, then, with obvious effort, her body relaxed. Her bare shoulders still tensed and the calm didn't reach her lightning gaze, but she regained her composure. "Is that what happened to you? Did someone leave?"

Rage reared up inside him. Belik often left their sessions annoyed but now there wasn't even any leadup. This had been building for days. "We talked about you," he snapped. "And how you chose to stay with people who hate you instead of joining something that matters."

"Something that matters?" All pretense was gone now. "The Tanyu are selfish, violent—"

"That doesn't sound like you?"

"—and I'll be glad when you're gone. All of you!"

For some reason, they were closer now, breathing hard. Light from the cloud-strewn sky outlined the shaved sides of her head, shadowed her lower lashes.

She lowered her voice. "You are terrified someone will discover your emptiness. That is why you don't answer my questions."

"I don't answer to you."

"No. You think it strength when you demean me, but you're too afraid to open up yourself. You're right. Perhaps I would laugh." She leaned close enough that he could feel her breath on his skin. "Perhaps I would pity you."

Belik couldn't breathe, choked with disbelieving anger. No one spoke to him like this. Not Tanyu, not enemies, not *katah* girls.

She stared at him coolly. "You're a fool and a coward."

His hand flashed up and he had her pinned against the wall before he knew what he was doing, hand on her neck. A shuddering blink was her only sign of surprise. She didn't struggle. The warm, soft skin of her throat didn't even work to breathe.

Slowly, she smiled, the septum ring settling into the bow of her lip.

Then she disappeared.

Chetana drew in a breath as she returned to her little room. The books had fallen again, though from what this time she couldn't tell. The blankets had been disarrayed, so perhaps she had thrashed or struggled in this room while she fought to stay calm with Master Belik.

Finally, she had made him show emotion. He would be dwelling on her for days now. She could even take a break from the constant focus.

The victory, however, tasted sour. *She just wanted to leave you.*

The cost of getting under his skin was allowing him to get under hers. It hadn't even been a choice. His impassive face, brutal and handsome and intelligent, wore away at her nerves. Never before had a target bothered her so intensely.

She was simply worn down. She'd created too many *katahs* in a row. That was enough to fray even the strongest person.

A fool and a coward she had called him. But was he? Belik feared he was, and that was enough.

With the rush subsiding, Chetana's shoulders sagged. She shook herself, ran one hand through her short curls, and went to find food to keep up her strength. The battle wasn't over yet.

***

A FLY CRAWLED across Sias Jairon's desk. How did a fly get in here?

Belik watched it as Sias folded his hands, blocking its path. The fly skittered sideways, flew in a bumbling pattern forward, and hummed to the far side of the room.

"There's no need for you to be constantly targeted without an organized counterattack," the Head was saying. "I assume you have been gathering intelligence about Original Plan?"

Belik cleared his throat and looked up. "Yes. We could just ask Gerand too. She was part of them."

"Years ago." Sias waved one hand dismissively. His knuckles looked knobbier than usual, crisscrossed with veins. "You can set up an interview but her information can only go so far. Only in the past few months has the group made such an effort to dismantle the Academy. I'd like you to find out why and whether we ought to prepare a counterstrike."

Whether we ought to? Of course they needed to destroy Original Plan. It was bent on the destruction of the Tanyu. What else was there to know?

"As you would have it," Belik replied.

"I see you haven't dealt with Chetana yet. I'm glad. Don't break the *katah* before you have a better grasp of their methods and goals."

"Master Jairon," Belik protested, unable to help himself, "we have all we need in Gerand. Trust me. This new one is maddening."

Sias leveled a look at him. "You're able to keep her talking, aren't you?"

"She doesn't talk about relevant things. It's all questions and accusations."

"She doesn't talk about herself?"

"Some imagined childhood. Clichés. Nothing we can use."

Sias made a noise in his throat. "This doesn't strike me as a difficult task for someone so Talented." His tone was soft but the meaning stung. He rose from his seat. "Now, I have some tests to oversee."

As Master Jairon left the room, Belik couldn't stop seeing Chetana's smug smile.

⸻

CHETANA WAITED two days to visit him again. Belik's Tanyuin pride wouldn't let him rest until he saw her, she knew. The thought of him tossing in the covers, unable to relax, brought her satisfaction.

He had come so close to killing her. If she hadn't kept her wits at the right moment, he might have done it. Oddly, part of her thought he wouldn't do it, that the strike was a warning. He had only held her there, after all, not squeezed out all her breath, which was cold comfort.

No one came to see her these days. She had to remain focused on her task, so others knew to stay away. Who would want to visit anyway? The family she'd found here, such as it was, had their own concerns. Besides, she knew she was unusual, not only for being a Khelê but also because she couldn't have fun like others did. Humor held little meaning for her. The women of Original Plan weren't typically jovial, but even among these, she sometimes felt exiled. A tool to be used for the cause until it broke and was replaced by another.

Then she would be useful. Crossing her legs under her and sitting straighter on the edge of the bed, she closed her eyes.

Belik was already there, no hint of apology in his eyes. And why should there be remorse? They were enemies. She had attacked him too, though in a different manner. For her part, she would never apologize either.

"We are back again," she forced herself to say.

For the cause, for the cause...

Exhaustion threatened to overwhelm her at the sight of him there, so solid, so indomitable. She'd won a point, but he looked fresh. Perhaps he never lost sleep after all. She bit her lip to distract from the bitterness.

"You don't want to do this, do you?" he asked, almost gentle.

The shift in his attitude took her aback. "I always want to be with you," she replied automatically, although her thoughts ran counter.

"Tell me the truth, and I'll tell you some too." He didn't smile, as another might, but there was new candor in his voice.

"That would be easy, wouldn't it?" she said, stalling. What was his game here? Was her mind so addled that she couldn't see the trap he was laying? Then she added, "I always tell you the truth."

Almost always. The cause mattered more than truth, more than life. But here the truth was like a precious fruit, delicious even when the skin had spines.

Belik hadn't told the truth the other day about Gerand. She was at the Academy. They probably had never even talked.

Still, he responded most when Chetana was honest, too tired to be otherwise. She'd fallen into old patterns of flattery, but maybe that wasn't the best method with this man.

She canted her head slightly, risking a step forward in the darkness. It took the shape of a gray and hazy room. She sharpened some of its edges. He liked when she did that.

"All right," she said. "I dislike you."

"I dislike you too."

"Honesty is a miracle," she said, barely veiling the sarcasm in her voice, but strangely relieved too. Precious fruit. "What don't you like about me?"

She'd heard it all. Mockery in the streets of King's Heights, complaints from her mother before she died, criticism from the others in Original Plan, her own inner voice, insisting that she hold herself to an impossible standard of perfection. Perfection had died with the first *katah* killing, but the remains of perfection called to her like voices of the dead.

"You hide your abilities."

Chetana blinked. "What do I—?"

"You can do more than you show. The Academy could have made some use of your Talent, not wasted it."

"I dislike your crassness," she bit back. "You have no respect for me or what I stand for."

"How can I respect you if you're trying to kill me? You didn't join a cause worth following."

"The unity of the Khelê, who have been persecuted and marginalized throughout their existence despite having a beauty and dignity that you yourself know is true? I want us to stand for more than violence and division. Can you say the same?"

"Yes," he said quickly. "We are more than that. We're skill. We're the best the world has to offer."

"Are you equating the Khelê with the Tanyuin Academy?"

Belik huffed, the muscles in his neck flexing. Maybe he'd been unaware of his travesty of logic.

"Truth for truth," she added, forcing her racing heart to slow. "Who gets to go next?"

Belik flew backward, blasted by light Chetana shot from her hands.

Black spots followed his eyes when he blinked at the hazy landscape. He put his glasses back in place before rising. In the Unreal, he didn't need them, but their presence was comforting, something to do with his hands while he thought. They made him feel like himself.

"Weak," he said. When had his tone become half-teasing?

Chetana lifted her chin, sure of herself. She glared down at him, dark eyes glittering in the light of the flying machines all around them. They ballooned like lanterns in the darkness, with baskets below that could lift ten people, though only the two of them stood in this one. Others he imagined filled with people on the inside too, not just in the hanging baskets. Real world logic didn't need to apply here. Weight didn't need to matter. People could fill the oval center of the machine like ants in a hill and it wouldn't careen off track unless he willed it.

Yes, he was showing off. So what? Goading Chetana to reveal the limit of her capabilities, and therefore Original Plan's, helped the Academy, and gave him a chance to stretch his mind in unusual directions. Sometimes an answer to a problem would come unbidden while he did these exercises.

Part of him insisted he was showing her too much. He shut it up. What was she going to do with the fact that he could create flying machines, turn into vapor, make the ground crumble away into an endless fall?

"Not bad," he amended.

Chetana cast an imperious glance at their surroundings. "Not terrible."

She liked the machines. A small, unwelcome warmth rose in his chest. Once she'd dropped the vacuous façade of open flirtation, he learned that Chetana was not easy to impress. Neither of them were.

"I learned that at fourteen," he said.

"Seventeen." She leaned back against the short barrier wall of the vessel. She wasn't ashamed of having learned the skill later than he had, but her spine remained straight. Never quite at ease.

He couldn't get her to fully relax, to believe. There had been times the past couple months when he could swear he'd done it, but then her eyes would light and her jaw would tense. She'd fight back. Without being fully in the moment, with him in the Unreal, they couldn't as easily get hurt.

"Your sister teach you that one?"

One of her eyebrows shifted upward in response. "No. I don't want you to talk about her."

"You do want me to. I can read your thoughts." It wasn't strictly true, but an educated guess could be as good as truth. He'd learned that in his brief time as Strategy Master. "She's a good Tanyu."

Chetana looked like she wanted to spit, but was above such things. He could barely even imagine her doing that, looking at her now with such taut control and dignity.

"That doesn't surprise me," she said. "Was it meant to?"

"No."

"Are you two close? Is she giving you instructions for how to talk to me?"

"No."

The breeze from their flight shuffled through her hair. Complicated shadows covered her face, highlighting her cheekbones. He realized he was adding more lights, taking them away, adjusting the angles. He stopped.

"We don't talk much," he said.

"You don't talk to anyone very often but me, do you?" Her voice had shifted. The comment wasn't an unusual move for a *katah*, but there was something in her tone —weakness was the first word that came to mind, then vulnerability—that made him think that the same must be true for her.

No comradery among Original Plan, then? That was finally something he could take back to Sias, beyond outlining the assumptions Chetana made while fighting. The way someone crafted a fight told Belik everything he needed to make a first impression.

Chetana wasn't impulsive. She waited, sometimes to her own hurt, for an opening. She wasn't fast moving, but thoughtful and powerful. One blow from her was worth three from rookie Tanyu who charged in too fast. She preferred to end a fight quickly if that was an option. Hence, the ball of light. Her repertoire of moves paled in comparison to any Tanyu, but for someone who seemed all but self-taught, she'd mastered those moves well. She had anger and determination and power and wisdom and patience. If she weren't a gory traitor, then she might have made a good ally.

"I don't," he admitted, answering her question. "And you're alone too. No one would care if I killed you now, would they?"

A rare glimpse of pain shone in her face for an instant before she covered it again. Her smooth brow furrowed and the corners of her lips stretched. Something deeply sad welled in her expression, like a distorted stone seen from above water. She blinked and the look was gone.

She was a professional killer, not a schoolgirl. He liked her better that way.

Belik came up short. When had he started liking anything about Chetana? She was infuriating, never coming any closer, always prodding into his past.

His cultivated hatred clicked back into place.

She pulled away from the barrier to stand proud as a queen on the other side of the landing. "If you haven't slain me already, you never will."

His annoyance had no sharp edges this time. She walked toward him slowly, fearless. Lights from the craft glowed along her muscled arms as she moved. The scent of sandalwood, her signature, wafted with her. Steel burned in her gaze. Not since the first night they met had she stood so close without violence, her body's warmth seeping into the tiny space between them. They glared at each other. He could reach out and grab her easily, as he had when he'd pushed her against the wall.

Proximity didn't matter as much in the Unreal—he could kill her as easily over there than close by—but the message was clear. *You'll never kill me.*

But he'd have to. Probably better sooner than later, the way things were going.

BELIK WAS GOING to kill her. It was the only way to explain why he suddenly started answering all her questions.

Yes, he didn't have many friends.

No, he didn't regret that.

Yes, he was proud of his position as Strategy Master.

No, not every campaign went as he expected.

No, he didn't expect to fail.

She tried harder, seeing how far she could make him go. He hedged actual revelations about himself. Any time he got too close, he'd step back, but only a little. He wanted them both to get closer to danger.

Yes, he grew up in the Western Kingdom.

Yes, he resented his father for leaving him alone so much.

Yes, the Tanyu gave him purpose.

No, he'd never fallen in love. He didn't know what that meant and suspected it was imaginary, a fiction for lives more boring than his own.

"You?" he asked brusquely.

"Have I ever fallen in love?" she clarified. "No. I agree that it's likely stories have propagated the myth until people deceive themselves."

Belik grunted agreement. He had a different sound for irritation, another for admitting that she'd made a point worth thinking about. He accused her of belying her intelligence, but he did the same. He measured out thoughts in grains when there were clearly fields within.

They fell silent.

Rain pattered steadily on the beach under a dark sky. They stood with their backs against impossible leafy trees, watching. A storm threatened in the distance, but never came closer. The silence was too comfortable. No, that descriptor fell short of the mark. It was not peace, but a truce. *He's going to kill you.*

She scrutinized his face, looking for signs that he would strike. She had stared at that face long enough now that she could read him well. A lifting of the muscular shoulders and a twist of the lips would forecast an imminent attack. The part of his wrist that showed beneath the black sleeves of his Tanyuin uniform would flex at the moment she should disappear back to her cavern room.

None of those things happened.

She relaxed a fraction. A childish part of her just wanted to *be* here with him. Neither victim nor aggressor. Just two people who knew the other had hideous elements holding them together but stayed anyway, with no agenda. They had both killed for opposing causes, and for that she would never forgive him. But he sought her out and told her truths, even cruel ones. For that, she felt a thread of gratefulness. For a connection forged in dissembling violence, theirs had become civil, even understanding.

This is where danger lies. It was in this moment that the opponent had most strength.

Chetana was the opponent.

The Tanyu had let down his guard. A fraction was all she needed. She let resolve fill her with the thought of her cause and how much she hated this man in front of her. His fights and evasions and the way he guessed at some of the only places that remained tender to the touch after training with Original Plan obsessed her days in the real world.

Now, all her tactics might actually work. It was her fierceness, not her allure, that won him to this false comfort in her presence.

"It's a myth people want to believe," she resumed, "because it's easier than accepting that one will be alone always."

"*Alone always*," he repeated with a touch of amusement. "Are you writing a poem? You always talk like that." To him, it was obviously frivolous.

Her heart hammered. "You like to pretend." She glanced around at the rain and the sand. He looked back at her when she met his gaze.

She would take a knife and... Breath failed her. Why was this any different than the other monsters she had slain? It wasn't. He wasn't.

She sidled close to him.

But he believed she had great ability, and he knew her sister, which few did. She had told him parts of their upbringing, how it dragged on, punctuated by rejection and piercing loneliness until Original Plan had taken them in as children. They gave Chetana food so she wouldn't starve. They showed her the harsh truth that brief militant action was required to bring peace to a race that had suffered. He knew and appreciated how serious-minded she was. He knew she still felt the pain of loneliness in her chest, but she wouldn't bend to petty worldliness when the future was at stake.

She kept one hand free as she snaked the other around his waist. He felt warm and firm, a pillar in her way. Images of the flying machines and the snowy forest and the dozens of other landscapes he'd created ran through her mind. She pressed her body against his. Raindrops dripped on them from above.

"Could we not pretend together?" she whispered, drawing close to his face. Her voice cracked on the last word and she swallowed.

His dilated pupils revealed his desire. His hands felt hot on her upper arms, a hold that could as easily push her away as pull her close.

Now, to choose the moment. He looked lost in her, but if she tried and failed, he would return the strike as fast as blinking. She had one chance. She flexed feeling back into her free hand, moving closer.

Belik surged forward to take her mouth with his. There was something harsh and primal about the way he kissed her. He acted as though she'd run if she could, and this was the only chance he'd have to claim her.

Chetana's thoughts scrambled among the sensations. The sharp scent of surf and their hands moving possessively over their bodies, a conversation of aversion and desire.

Now! Do it now. She felt herself losing awareness of the Unreal. The rough hilt of a knife formed under her palm, bringing her mind back enough so that he couldn't take her by surprise. But it was too late for that. He wanted her.

She gripped the knife hard. One blow to the heart or the neck. She could stab him again and again if she had to.

His rough skin rasped against her cheek and chin. The kiss was too honest, more than she'd planned.

We could pretend. The lonely child inside her insisted that she let him kiss and pretend it wasn't the best time to finish her mission.

She pulled back the knife. Voices roared in her ears. Sensible voices and desperate, all calling for her to jump. This was the crux, the moment of choice, and she could not go back.

Gasping, she stopped and brought her face away from his. With effort, she stopped the rain and turned the surf red.

He'd know where he was. He would not die today.

Something small and cold fizzed against the skin of her shoulder. Snow. Dazed, she looked up. Red snow. She hadn't made that. It could have been lovely if it didn't carry with it the sense of horror. It was still lovely.

She looked down at Belik again. He stared at the knife still in her hand. It vanished into dust.

The truth hit them both like a body blow. Belik had been quicker to get rid of his weapon, but they had both been about to complete the *katah*. At the last second, he created snow and she created red surf, signals to the other that they were in the Unreal.

He'd saved her from himself, and she'd done the same.

The next moment was a desperate scramble of nails and lips, angry and intense. They hurt each other and didn't care. Belik growled, feral. Her shirt was torn, getting it off.

When they finished, the waves were blackish-blue. They looked perfectly real.

THE FOLLOWING WEEKS passed in an array of dazzling locations and aggressive passion. Afterwards, they'd both get caught off guard for a tiny bubble of time when nothing seemed to matter, lying there, and Chetana knew she shouldn't say the things she did. Like the fact that the other Original Plan members ostracized her, and she missed her sister. After a particularly acid interaction with Maal, Chetana enjoyed the torrent of abuse that Belik poured out on her behalf. When was the last time someone had stood up for her?

But she still hated him for being Tanyu. He too must be balanced on the line between love and hate. The problem was that both emotions focused on him even more, seething or longing. His mind always turned toward her too, and whenever it did, she was there.

Belik might sometimes hate her, but he saw her. He saw her ability and her passion. He liked her seriousness and even her crimes. For some reason, he found her irresistible.

She had completed *katahs* in the past, but none of them felt like this. In those, she was always in charge, as though she stood on a rock in the middle of a swirling ocean sucking down her victims. The intimacy was strategic, almost mechanical, as though she were performing choreography. Through acid smiles and sultry words, she herself managed to stay untouched by anything but a sticky veneer left behind by their addiction.

And that was enough to hurt.

Even after those connections, she felt sick and weak for days, staying in bed, shrugging off the horrific sense that her own skin had been peeled away when she killed them.

This—*this*—was different. The things Belik loved and hated about her mirrored what she loved and hated about herself. His memories felt like her own, their shouting matches sounded like the voices in her own head. And always there was the anticipation of more. More understanding of him, of herself. More explosively imaginative worlds he'd show her. More pride in the fierce capability they both had and the knowledge that they should kill each other but wouldn't. They were rebels in a private world.

They lay in an enormous hammock in the bowels of a

wooden ship so large that the fasteners above them were barely visible. Green and yellow striped blankets draped over them. The gentle sway of the huge vessel lulled her down into an unguarded drowsiness.

Beside her, Belik stared at the distant ceiling, bare arms behind his head. His sharp eyes didn't need glasses here, though he wore them in the Real. She watched his gaze shift in tiny movements. His forehead grew furrowed again, the haze of satisfaction already wearing off. He'd leave soon.

"What are you thinking about?" she asked quietly.

Dust glowed in faint beams of light across their nest. Often, she could tell his thoughts—when he was planning what to tell the Tanyuin Head or when he was thinking about her. Now he was opaque, and she wanted to break him open.

The quality of silence skewed sideways. They hadn't talked about the decision not to complete their missions with an assassination. It was understood. The ramifications already nipped at Chetana's heels.

Months had passed, and all she had were excuses and slivers of information.

Belik dreamed of being the Tanyuin Head, but his obsession with her would jeopardize that.

Chetana stiffened. Did they finally need to talk about the lie they'd woven? She didn't know what she could say. Desire had become necessity, something that went beyond like and dislike. Panic surged up in her gut as Belik let the silence drag out longer, but she forced it down.

"Could you get to Tarryall?" His voice sounded huskier than usual.

"Where is that?" Surely, he wasn't revealing the position of the Tanyuin Academy? As soon as the thought crossed her mind, it sounded ridiculous.

Belik explained Tarryall was two days out from Rantoul, a town north of King's Heights.

Her breath squeezed thin and she reached for his arm, drawing one hand lazily along its scars, trying to hide how tense her own muscles felt. "Perhaps," she answered.

With a sudden movement, he twisted to look at her, angling on his elbow. His eyes burned with unreadable emotion. "We should meet. This isn't good enough."

Chetana's skin felt covered in static. She felt her eyes go wide, her lips part in shock. Dimly, she thought of the cause she'd devoted her life to, the one she still believed in unto death, but it felt so far away from this moment.

"No."

The voice was hers but her mind didn't belong to it. She watched herself answer, watched Belik's lip curl slightly, eyes narrow. A muscle in his jaw jumped. And for just a moment, hurt flashed in his expression. Anger quickly covered it, but it was there, not imagined.

"When?" she amended, inhabiting her body again.

"Three weeks."

Air wouldn't stay in her lungs. Her gut dropped as though she fell from a great height, arms and legs flailing, but so free in the open air.

Her mouth wouldn't form the word she wanted. Instead, she groped like a blind woman for Belik's hand. Their grip, when they intertwined fingers, was too strong, painful.

She inhaled slowly. *This is not Real.* The pain eased. And she knew what she would say.

"Yes."

THE VILLAGE of Tarryall was close to nothing. It looked like an accident sprung out of the woods. No main roads crossed it; no towering structures gave it any image of power. It was just a hamlet one needed a map to find.

Sias didn't often send Belik on missions, but this time he said he wanted him to investigate a rash of new people with the Talent that came from this backwater.

Belik scowled. Chetana arrived here before him and told him where to go, since neither of them knew the territory. Where was he supposed to find a gory white house around here? Everything looked brown. Brown wood, brown trees, brown streets. His gaze snagged on a building to his right. White paint dotted the doorframe. His heartbeat quickened.

White house. Could that be it? It would be like Chetana to play such a trick. Scanning the desolate road one more time for anything white, he concluded it had to be here. Her presence was everywhere in this town, buzzing beneath his skin like wine, like heat, like a stream of life he could drink from.

He turned his mind and body toward the little building, no more than a hayloft, really, set back from the one main road. His blood was fire. No sounds echoed from inside. At a touch of the handle, the door swung inward on squeaky hinges, not even latched.

The space within looked empty, bare wooden walls (some of which had speckles of whitewash like the lintel,) a loft area above, square-cut beams standing like sentinels at intervals. The smell of it reminded him of his youth and he snuffed the dusty scent out of his nose. One corner of the ground floor looked lived in. Maybe a squatter, maybe a dedicated farmer, lived here. There was a mattress in one corner and a washtub, along with a meager number of personal effects, including a linen shirt hanging from a peg.

Fear spiked through him, unexpected and unwanted. Was he

in the right place? Would she look as she did in his dreams? Would he even recognize her? Would all this subterfuge be worth it? Did she lure him here to mock him?

"You're an hour late." Her rich, musical voice sounded through the room.

He turned around. By the door stood Chetana, tall as a queen, dark and soft and fierce. Those Khelê tattoos on her shaved head had been no illusion. He could have cut himself on them and bled.

She clicked the door shut and bolted it behind her. Her dark eyes were liquid and fire at once.

All the times she'd tormented him flooded back and mixed with his desire. He ran at her and slammed her against the wall. She was real beneath him, grabbing for the hem of his shirt. He pinned her with the weight of his body and grabbed her wrists to stop her, capturing them against the splintering wood of the loft.

She snarled, head back, and leveled a look at him so vicious that he had to silence it, to aggravate it, to partake in it. He kissed her with the fury he'd felt all these months. She returned the kiss, twisting out of his hold and shoving him back. She caught him by the collar with one hand and kept them pressed against each other as they fought.

His breath caught as he tripped backward. Anger rising, he saw that she had tripped him deliberately, had swept her leg to catch his. He grabbed her upper arms hard enough to leave bruises. Her strong muscles moved under the skin as she tried once again to tug at his shirt. This time he let her take it off.

He was king and slave. What he wanted, and what he deserved for his sins. It didn't last long enough.

In the aftermath, a light sheen of sweat shone on the bare sides of her head. He dragged his thumbs over her eyes, her cheeks, her lips. They were impossibly soft for someone so fierce. She had hidden nothing in the Unreal. Chetana was the Unreal come to life.

They clothed themselves again in a silence that became pointed in its permanency. Was there anything to say? They had wanted each other and had each other and could never have each other permanently. It was that frustration made them consume every minute. Even now, he felt time slipping out of his grasp. *Not yet.*

"You're just the same," Belik said, shouldering his long Tanyuin coat.

Chetana eyed him as she buckled her shoes. "And so are you." She pointed to a long, thin scar on his calf. "Except for this. Where did you get this?"

"A cat did it." He put his glasses back on and raised an eyebrow at her, daring her to disbelieve him.

Her mouth curled in a smile. Did they ever really believe each other? She ran a finger lightly along the scar.

It wasn't the Unreal. It was simpler and better, worse and more complicated all at once. He captured her hand with his own and kissed the back of it. He'd never been romantic, but then he'd never cared about anyone.

He gave her a kiss without violence, touching the tender spot beneath her jaw.

He wanted to stay and talk like they did in the Unreal. This loft didn't seem part of reality anyway. But he didn't know what to say. His strategic mind had gone hazy with pleasure.

"Again," he said stupidly, standing up. "We'll do this again."

Chetana remained sitting. "I'm not certain I can get away." The sincerity in her tone made her seem suddenly young. Before, she was ageless, an undying queen. And now, she wasn't the monster that haunted his dreams, just a girl, twenty years old, who would never be his.

A bad time to realize that he didn't just need her. He

liked her.

"I have the freedom to travel." Mostly true. "I'll meet you somewhere." Meeting in King's Heights sounded vile. It was far from the Academy, though she didn't know it. But if it meant more of this, then his conscious, thinking brain would step aside in favor of whatever would make it happen.

———

CHETANA LAY on her stomach in bed, reading one of the books Gerand had left behind. The words slid by, unattached to meaning.

Two months had passed, and she still had no blood.

For weeks, she'd ignored the truth, but it grew as certainly as the child in her belly. What could she do now? The clammy dread of discovery had made her thoughts foggy.

Every excuse she used to cover her relationship with Belik was wearing thin. Tired from living so long underground, she needed a short break to see a childhood friend, she'd explained before traveling to Tarryall. The fresh air would give her renewed energy to finish her mission.

She told them she felt sick, but her sickness had persisted beyond what was normal. She said it would only take a couple more weeks and then she would finish the mission and kill the Tanyuin strategist.

If only no one would bother her, so she could figure out what kind of life to live now that she was hurdling toward motherhood. Pregnant by an enemy. It was the stuff of sordid stories, something she should transcend, but she hadn't. She couldn't. He was part of her.

Now, the other members cast her suspicious looks when she emerged from her room to eat, though they could not know the extent of her betrayal.

Women who had cared for her, even other specials like herself, now regarded her as something tainted. Whispering stopped when she entered rooms. No one had openly confronted her yet about her six-month *katah*, but they would. Then what could she tell them?

The door to her room opened, sending a shudder through her. Every noise meant the end, that someone had discovered her. They would assume that she didn't want the Tanyuin Academy destroyed. She still did want that. She wanted it with so much of herself that she ached.

Maal's familiar form filled the doorway. Chetana rolled up to sitting, placing her finger between pages to mark the place she had stopped reading.

"Feeling better today?"

As soon as Chetana nodded, sickness heaved up in her gut. She straightened convulsively to keep it down. The grip on her book tightened.

Maal's sharp eyes took in the little gestures. Her warrior instincts clearly saw that something was wrong. "Good," she replied. "Have you made any progress with your mark?" Without waiting for an answer, she tilted her head back. "How long has it been? This one must be a slippery man. Or a handsome one." Her gaze locked onto Chetana's.

She kept her expression even. "He is one of the most powerful people among their kind. His training is second to none. That I live is testament to how I am progressing."

A tense quiet settled, but Chetana had a lifetime of experience with that. She simply waited.

Finally, Maal said, "Well, he must trust you by this point, then."

Chetana didn't respond. Bile kept burning her throat.

"I look forward to the day when his death brings us closer to victory," Maal continued.

"As do I."

Maal sighed, her posture relaxing a little. She lowered her voice. "You don't seem well. I can have Dilly bring you hyrax stew."

This time, Chetana couldn't stop it. She managed to throw the book backward onto the bed before she vomited on the floor.

***

"They kicked her out."

Across from Belik, Sias Jairon peaked his fingers and hummed thoughtfully. His usual expression, almost scholarly, had gained an edge of calculation. "She's no longer part of Original Plan?"

Last night, Chetana had told Belik that the other members disowned her, kicked her out of the only group where she'd ever belonged. If he didn't have to be here, he would have gone to her himself.

"I know we never send a second invitation but—"

"You of all people should understand why we can't send one to her."

Frustration bubbled inside him. "Master Jairon, she has the skills."

"I know that. I also know that her aim is to kill my Strategy Master."

This was the difficult part. To tell Sias without really telling him what was going on between him and Chetana. Belik's heartbeat pounded hard in his chest.

"Victories aren't only physical, but mental," he began. "You know this. We could kill them all—*will*, eventually—but a blow like this would discourage a similar group to form again. Chetana wouldn't be a martyr to rally behind."

"You've told me," Sias said slowly, "that she isn't well liked among the other members. If she has been disowned, as you say, then it will not matter to them what she does. And it doesn't matter to us either. She can provide us with no updated information. She's just a liability."

"I disagree." His face felt flushed. "She has no loyalty to them now, and her skills could aid us in taking them down."

Sias eased back in his seat. The knowing look he gave brought an uncomfortable twist to Belik's gut.

"What?" he growled.

"I've known you a long time, Belik. It wouldn't have bothered you to eliminate an enemy before. What's so special about this girl?"

Belik pursed his mouth. *Nothing. Everything.* There was no way he was spilling his guts to the Tanyuin Head, not when the man held the power to demote him or to make him his successor.

"Nothing besides the Talent. She has more than any non-Tanyu I've met."

"And you've met many non-Tanyu?"

Belik could have punched the smug look off Sias's face. He ground his teeth. "Fine. Lose an asset. Gore!"

Sandalwood breathed through his mind.

"I'll kill her if you want," he finished. "Gory waste."

"I think that would be best," Sias agreed.

"As you would have it." The words felt stuck in his throat, but somehow they managed to come out as he hurried from the room.

Belik walked through the halls of the Academy as he checked for Chetana in the Unreal. She waited for him. Warmth flooded his body.

She looked worn, but otherwise the same. He didn't ask what was wrong. Often, they visited each other just to exist in a place that made them feel alive and seen. She'd come even more than usual the past few days. It was constant. She was his flesh and blood, his mind and soul.

"You have a place to sleep tonight?" he asked, when she didn't say anything.

"I'll manage," she said dismissively, as though it were obvious. Her skin grew ashier with the answer, though. She was suffering, and the feeling pervaded him too. He wasn't just testy with Sias but with everyone else. People were starting to notice he wasn't merely gruff, but short-tempered and volatile.

Around them, colors started to swirl in the black in thick ribbons. The two of them floated among the display, suspended. For a while they watched the dancing rainbows, the slithering greens and shooting yellows.

"Belik," she said, coming nearer. Her voice was so low he could barely hear it. "When can we meet again?"

The question wasn't seductive or demanding, but heartbreakingly vulnerable. It made him almost afraid, ready to replace the walls he'd started to dismantle around the fragile parts of himself.

"Depends," he grunted. He hadn't seen her in person more than the one time, and that was three months ago now. It felt safer not to be drawn too far into her. But it was too late for that. Chetana was everything he wanted to be and have. Switching tack, he stroked her head and brought his hand down to massage her shoulder. The well-knit muscles there began to relax.

"I need to see you," she whispered.

Glowing red bands of light flowed between them, briefly illuminating their faces. As if that were a reminder of the space still between them, she closed the gap, wrapping her arms around his waist.

Yes, she'd lost Original Plan, but was that why she seemed so sad now? Maybe sad was the wrong word. She seemed almost anxious. Chetana wasn't fearful. It was one of his favorite things about her. She'd charge at the front of an army if she had to, metal racing through her veins.

"What do you need to tell me?" he asked. "We can do it here, not wait a month."

"Do you not want to see me again?"

Belik swore, releasing her. "We're past this. You know I do. What is it?" This damned nervousness was beginning to infect him too.

Her eyes flashed fire, criticizing him for letting her go.

There she was. It was a relief to see her strength again.

"I need your kindness, Belik," she snapped.

He didn't have much, he knew, but he mustered what he could, even as he tensed for a blow. Their surroundings already felt like kindness, like vulnerability. This was where he went to be alone, when his responsibilities left him breathless.

He kissed her full lips. "There." He tried to smile, but the attempt fell flat. "Now, what is it? If members of Original Plan are after you, you know I'll kill them for you." There was no need to offer it, since Chetana was a warrior in her own right.

She shuddered. The movement was barely there, but with his hand on her arm, he felt it. "No. They're not. They would never treat me that way."

Unlikely. "Then what?" He couldn't rein in his patience much longer.

"They didn't make me leave because I told them about our situation. They abandoned me because they found out for themselves."

Abandoned. The word struck a painful chord behind his ribcage. But then the rest of the sentence seeped in, gradual understanding beginning to dawn. "Found out," he repeated, his eyes lowering to her abdomen.

She nodded stoutly, her inner armor back in place. "Yes." The word came out angry. "I have your child."

Sound muffled to nothing. Breath suspended. It felt as if his very organs stopped, frozen in a patch of timelessness. Thoughts without words pinged harmlessly against his consciousness, each clambering to be heard, but he was unreachable.

"Our child," he choked. "You're pregnant."

She rubbed her lips together and nodded.

"Bastards," he said. Ideas came through in a rush. The first was that the people Chetana cared about would abandon her over this. "Bastards!"

"Don't curse them," she said.

"I want him," he burst out. That it was a son and that their son would have the Talent felt as inevitable as sunrise.

A smile transfigured Chetana's face. She didn't smile often, and he floated dumbfounded.

"I want him too," she said, laying one hand on her belly.

The shock started to give way to an almost manic excitement, even happiness. He stifled a hysterical laugh, as he counted up from their encounters in Tarryall. "He's due in early spring?"

"Early spring," she confirmed.

This baby couldn't exist. Belik couldn't have him, but Chetana and now this child were like the Unreal, an Unreal just for him, as bright and as full of possibility. Surely there was a way that Chetana could live in Tánuil, the town adjacent to the Academy, if Sias didn't change his idiotic mind and let her into the Academy where she belonged.

"I'll come see you." It didn't matter how it was done. He fantasized about meeting her all the time, but Academy work had kept him busy. Maybe the Head had sensed his transformation after the trip to Tarryall and made sure to give him jobs that kept him up late at night.

"That was all my request, stubborn man." Her voice was teasing, lighter than it had been.

"Infuriating woman."

They reached for each other. The glowing colors circled them in a cyclone of light.

THIS TIME IT WAS REDSHORE, not Tarryall.

The baby wrapped his chubby hand around Chetana's finger as she sat with a book in the other hand. This one was an excerpt from the Sacred Scroll about the founding of Brithnem, the capital of the Western Kingdom. She'd read parts of it, since Khelê history was so firmly connected to the story, but this version was her own. She'd found a copy in Grand Market Square, bound in blue fabric. It had called to her immediately.

Redshore lay north of the capital, where she now lived. Khelê weren't persecuted there as they were in King's Heights. She could move without fear, though her sister-members never lay far from her thoughts. Yes, they had abandoned her when they'd learned about the pregnancy, but wouldn't she have done the same only a year ago? Everyone but Belik had abandoned her, and now this child, whom she loved like life.

He gargled and shook the finger he held. Chetana smiled, smoothing his thin hair back over light, soft skin. Her son could pass for Kingdom, but that was one of the unique gifts of the Khelê. Offspring didn't match their parents. Often, they had what many ignorant people called deformities or abnormalities. At a minimum they would have different skin tones or body types. Secretly, she'd hoped her son would be more obviously Khelê, but she adored him despite his orthodox appearance.

She turned back to the passage from the Sacred Scroll. *The*

Khelê demonstrate the multifarious grace of God, it said. *It is not outward appearance, nor ability, nor bloodline that makes them worthy.* The words sang in her blood. Khelê existed to reveal the true worth of an individual. One day, she'd memorize this passage and pass it onto her son. Brithnem had programs that taught the entire Scroll, which she didn't have the means to purchase.

The baby began fussing and she closed the book, tucking it into her bag. She shooed away an insect buzzing around her son's face. Now there was little to distract her save the soft crashing of waves down the beach.

Today, finally, she'd see Belik again in the flesh.

Their attempts to meet kept getting thwarted by his allegiance to the Tanyuin Academy. In seven months, they'd only seen each other one other time. This was the first time he would meet his son.

She swallowed away the dryness in her mouth. Though she had long intended to convince him to leave the Academy, she had never asked him. With her son in her arms, looking back at her with round, gray eyes, the possibility finally felt real. Belik would leave. They would live together in Brithnem, in secret if necessary.

"Chetana."

Her head snapped up. There he was, all in black. The dying light cast soft illumination over him, muting the martial outline of his figure.

She rose from her chair and stepped across the coarse grasses and sand. He wore his long Tanyuin coat, a stark contrast to her marigold skirt. His face was frozen, staring at their son. Something warmed in Chetana as the stare gave way to a wondering smile. At this moment, they were a family—a strange, fierce, accidental, necessary family, and she couldn't imagine another.

"Daelon, this is your father," she said. The baby goggled at Belik, head wobbling as Chetana held him steady.

"Chetana," Belik breathed, not taking his eyes off Daelon. His mouth moved with other words, but none gained precedence. He finally closed his mouth and stroked the baby's cheek.

Chetana smiled. "He is perfect."

Belik grunted asset. His gaze shifted from Daelon to her. "I wanted to be here more. I wanted you, but I couldn't get away."

"I know." She inhaled carefully. "You... were raised in Redshore, were you not?"

They both knew she was right.

"Daelon and I have made a good life in Brithnem. It's a beautiful city, with acceptance for Khelê and opportunities for him." She shrugged the arm holding Daelon. "All he lacks is his father."

Belik's answer came out quickly. "Don't blame me for not being able to come more often. I'm defying orders to see you at all." His eyes blazed. "And I do, I want you. Both. But don't ambush me to demand what I can't do for you."

Chetana's body hardened. "I'm not ambushing you. We would be better together. Of course I would ask!"

"We're together all the time."

"In the Unreal."

"Yes."

"Daelon can't be there with us."

"He will, in time."

"And what if he can't?"

Belik stiffened as if struck. "Of course he will."

"Even if he can, it will be years before his abilities manifest."

"As soon as they do, I'll send him a letter."

She squared her jaw. Images of a hearth fire and a too-large bed played through her thoughts. No, the Academy had already taken her sister and her lover. It couldn't have her son.

"He will not receive a letter," she said quietly, in a way Belik couldn't misunderstand. She would sooner see an Academy invitation burn than see it in the hands of her son.

"He will. You'll come too."

This was becoming out of hand. Against her instincts, she set the baby down on a blanket laid out on the sand and came nearer to Belik. She would end the Tanyuin Academy, or at least Belik's involvement in it, before she ever considered attending it herself.

She kissed him, soft and then more hungrily. He felt good, solid. Urgency for her new mission rose up strong as a battle cry. He must leave the Academy for them.

She pulled away, longing for more, but fearing to lose herself. Now she had her son to consider too.

"I will not." The words were clear. "I would never go to that filthy place."

His hand shot up under her jaw before she could move away. "Don't insult me. I came all this way to see my son, and you could only hope to get into the Tanyuin Academy."

She yanked her head away, jaw throbbing. Her gaze flicked to the baby before returning to Belik. "You have admitted to me yourself that I'm as Talented as many there. What need have I for a group dedicated to violence?" She lifted her hand in a vague but unmistakable gesture toward her chin. Desperation threatened low in her gut. She was losing him. "I do not want to fight."

"You always want to fight."

That was not strictly true. She breathed hard in the ocean air. The sky had gotten darker already, but the anger in Belik's face hadn't softened. He was so proud of his group, even more than she'd been proud of hers, because he thought there was little else in him to be proud of. He was flawed and alone as she was flawed and alone.

Little by little, her breathing steadied. "Please come with us," she said, satisfied that her voice came out with no apology or entreaty.

Belik scoffed. Then, amending, he said, "I want to be with him, but your fantasy can never happen. It's ridiculous. The only way we can be together is if you come to the Academy. I've known it since the beginning."

"The only way unless you are willing to leave a broken institution, you mean?" she said, lifting her chin.

Belik ground his teeth. "I won't leave."

"You would not leave for Daelon, or for me?"

Belik's chest rose and fell heavily, pain writ clearly in his features. If Chetana were one to apologize, she would have been tempted, although she'd done nothing wrong.

"No," he finally said, "and I don't have to."

"You do."

A fierce ache tore through Chetana's limbs. These words had to be said, but was there a way they didn't turn into an ultimatum he could refuse? *Why* was he refusing? Was the Tanyuin Academy so important that he could tear his own life apart to keep that paltry sliver of it?

She, for her part, would create a good life in Brithnem with her son, with or without him. Her mind stuttered at the thought, the implications. She couldn't live without Belik. Or it would barely be life. She'd had enough *katahs* to know how much they hurt, the invisible scars they left that never went away, even for a more trivial mark. This would be torture. Could she even care for her son properly if Belik were torn away from her?

Belik glared back at her, body vibrating with tension as she realized hers was too. Even in this, they were linked. "I won't leave," he said.

We can meet in the Unreal. This does not have to end. It cannot.

"You must if you want us." A salty sting of rage bit at the corners of her eyes.

"Chetana." It was less a word and more a rumbled warning.

"Belik."

For a heart-dropping second, neither of them moved. *Please.* The moment stretched, thin to breaking. Her own pain and anger reflected back in his burning gaze.

"I love you," she said, voice hoarse. "I want you here."

That caught him off guard. He blinked, but didn't back away. "Don't make me choose between you and the Academy."

All their words fell into the void opening between them, meaningless in the face of certainty.

Like a current, her distress flowed stronger and stronger. When it overflowed, Chetana shoved him hard. Surprised, he stumbled back a step.

"Don't make me choose," he snarled again.

"You have already made your choice." Fierce tears fell against her cheeks now.

"If you're so gory stubborn," he said, stalking back toward her, "you can live this pitiful life, with no one to take care of you, nobody to even know where you live, but you're not dooming our son to your mediocrity!"

She realized his intention a moment before he moved. "No!" she cried, stepping between Belik and Daelon. "He stays with me."

"What, will you make him a gory Amir? I saw what you were reading when I walked up."

"Perhaps I will. At least he won't be violent and cruel like his father."

"I'll be dead before I see him become a worthless, sniveling—"

Years of training in the caverns came back to her, made her arms shoot out, spin around, pinning Belik's arm behind his back. She didn't have a plan, but Daelon... She would do anything at all to protect him.

"Don't." The voice didn't even sound like hers.

With a roar, he launched himself backward against her. His weight threw her off balance. The wind expelled from her lungs as they landed hard on the ground. Scrambling up, she faced him again. This time he had a dagger in his hand. Moonlight slid along its blade.

Daelon began to cry, distressed by their commotion. Her heart bled for him. Perhaps that would literally be true in moments. She cast up a prayer for her soul.

Drawing back her shoulders, she curled her lip. "You need me."

Months of closest observation let her see Belik's fleeting hesitation. Was their *katah* strong enough to kill them both if he struck her? Daelon would be left an orphan.

Casting aside any other consideration, she hurled herself forward with a cry. A horrible wet crack sounded through the dark. Belik didn't scream when his leg broke at the knee. He simply fell backward on the sand with a gasp.

She clambered upright, out of range of the knife he still held in his fist. The soft sand thwarted her speed as if she lived in a bad dream. She did. "Devil," she spat.

He threw the dagger in response. She curled herself around the baby as the weapon sailed over her head.

Seconds later, the pain in her shoulder registered. It might be broken too. But she could run with one broken shoulder. Belik couldn't readily follow.

She left the blanket and the bag, gathered up the baby, and ran, angry sobs threatening to slow her progress. Curses followed her into the darkness.

SHIT!

Belik dragged himself by his arms farther away from the water. The stabbing pain in his leg was enough to make his vision narrow and throw off his aim.

She had done this. His mind was in chaos. She had done this and then she'd left him. The solution was so simple and he'd wanted it with a purity that frightened him. He analyzed weaknesses every day, so why couldn't he acknowledge how much the gory woman meant to him? Was this her plan from the beginning—not to kill him but to ruin him? Because now Sias would know what happened. Belik couldn't will this injury away, and he was too far from the city to get help quickly. He wouldn't be Tanyuin Head now, not with this stain on his record and his *katah* still alive. Maybe he could explain what happened some other way. Maybe this wouldn't affect his chances...

He sneered, arms shaking with the effort of holding himself together. It was as though he would explode if he didn't concentrate.

His son! His son! His chest ached at the thought of his little face. Belik needed to train him, to watch him grow powerful. With parents like his, he could be the greatest Tanyu ever seen.

A city of dreams came crashing mercilessly into the ocean. A life with Chetana, with his son, as Tanyuin Head. He dwelled on those images every day, caressing them, treating them gently before putting them away. And now they lay in hideous rubble.

Insulting, stubborn, gory woman. He'd get even. One day, he'd kill her. But even now the thought stabbed him with new pain.

"Shit."

THEY WOULD HAVE TO HIDE.

Chetana had lost the strongest connection she would ever

have with another human being. She wasn't one to dwell on the unfairness of life, but the weight of all her loneliness oppressed her senses until she could barely tell where she was going. Somehow, a day later, she arrived at the place where they were staying. She couldn't call it home.

A hollow had been carved out of her so large that she could have been trapped in a cage and felt freer. Now, she didn't know who or what she was. The horrific sound replayed in her head. What had she done?

What had to be done.

She and Belik had begun by hating each other. Some of that hatred had never left.

She looked down at Daelon, sleeping now. His bell-shaped mouth hung open, his lashes resting on his cheeks. She would not regret loving Belik, if only for Daelon's sake, but every drop of love had dried. Her life, apart from her son, would be penance for her sins. Even now, she felt Belik in the corner of her mind, but she would never go there again. Because of his wickedness, the Unreal was closed to her.

An idea slowly broke through the haze of shock and pain. Perhaps she could request to join the Amiran Academy herself. There was no need to wait until Daelon was old enough. Yes, part of the idea came from cold spite, but there was warm curiosity too. Books enough to fill a lifetime, wisdom to replace her foolishness, an occupation beyond regret. She would need time to heal before such an endeavor, but it could be a path forward. She would make a path forward, whether there or somewhere else.

Without Belik, she would live a fraction of a life. He was too ingrained, deep in her pores, in her blood. But she had always been a warrior. This time, she would fight for her own soul.

7

KINGDOM BUSINESS

SOME BELIEVED that Navigators could read the future as well as the stars.

Kiria doubted it. If they could, she would ask when full meals would replace the rations she'd established to deal with the food shortage. Three weeks of meager portions had made her people openly discontent, and she could hardly blame them.

She looked into the milk-white eyes of the elderly man in front of her, almost luminous in the darkness. Night wind breathed past, sharp and searching. Lights from the palace behind them glowed faintly.

Beside Kiria, Princess Haved radiated excitement, although most wouldn't be able to tell. Haved had already met several Navigators from the Night Colony of Qib, but to her they were celebrities who could teach her something new.

Too bad this one was a liar.

"Explain slowly what you saw," Kiria said, glancing upward at the sky. "If you could point it out, I would be grateful."

The lines in the man's dark face deepened. He worked his jaw as though chewing, looking down, instead of up at the stars that were causing so much trouble.

Behind him stood members of the shipping conglomerate that he worked for, signified by a diagonal sheaf of wheat sliced through with a deep X. Five men, all here to negotiate with the Keepers about importing necessary food for Brithnem's citizens. There would be a terrible shortage for a couple years due to the fires that signaled the beginning of the Tanyuin coup. That had been at the end of the summer, terrible timing for farmers who depended on the harvest.

On top of that blow, this company, capable of staving off hunger for her people almost single-handedly, now demanded that Kiria eliminate all tariffs on incoming goods. The Western Kingdom needed food, yes, but it also needed money to rebuild. There was no way she could lose that tax money, much of which she planned to use as stipends for the farmers who had lost their lands.

The Navigator shivered.

Haved said something softly to him in Charäkhni, and the man glanced behind him for permission before nodding back.

"A thicker jacket?" Kiria guessed in an undertone.

"Yes." Haved called forward a palace guard and instructed him to find something to make the Navigator more comfortable.

Haved wasn't only here for curiosity's sake. All the importers came from a rural area of Charäkhnem, her home kingdom. Large with the heir to the Western Kingdom's throne, Haved represented new friendship between the two countries. Not only did Kiria hope that Haved's presence would remind them that Charäkhnem was her ally, but it would also prevent them from having private conversations in a language Kiria didn't understand. Haved was her implicit translator.

"Lady Kiria," said one of the businessmen, dressed impeccably in a white silk tunic, "this exercise seems designed to keep us all in the cold." His tone was immaculately pleasant, but Kiria merely leveled a look at him.

Scaffolding covered sections of the palace inside and out. Sounds of construction and restoration rang through the hallways day and night. So, it was true that she conducted many of her meetings outside these days, despite the chilly winter breezes. This meeting, in particular, she didn't mind hosting in the cold.

"I am a person who enjoys the truth, Tamirat Izal. Here I'm simply looking for confirmation."

"Do you doubt the word of my Navigator?" Standing next to Izal, a man with a trimmed goatee chuckled lightly as if the man had told a joke.

The other three from the company stirred as though they'd been caught sleeping. Kiria had seen many reactions to her Beauty, and this one was common until people got used to seeing her.

"I doubt anyone who says I am an ill-fated ruler."

A jacket appeared for the Navigator, which prevented Izal's response. Kiria shifted her attention back to the elderly man wrapping the heavy coat around himself like a cape.

"Thank you," he said. "I wear it with pride." His accent was unlike any other Kiria had heard, a rich mix of several at once. His words rang almost like an apology.

"Now," Kiria said, wasting no time, "which stars claim that I am fated to 'cast the Kingdom into confusion'? Those were your words, weren't they?"

The loose skin at the man's neck wobbled as he swallowed. "Those are the words exactly." He took a couple hard blinks, staring steadfastly ahead, even though Kiria knew the lights from the palace, dim as they were from this distance, must be hurting his eyes. Navigators worked better in complete darkness.

"Lady Kiria," Izal resumed, "does it matter which stars Dev points out to you? Excuse me, but does My Keeper know the stars?"

"I do," Haved chimed in. She couldn't read the future in them, but she knew more constellations than Kiria did. Kiria was glad she didn't clarify.

Izal bowed his head. "Of course you do, my princess."

Dev the Navigator seemed to take this as his cue to do something. His ghostly eyes finally sought the sky, tentative, as though he'd wronged it. Kiria's certainty in her own hunch solidified. The importers had created this rumor to blackmail her into capitulating.

"When you're ready," Kiria prompted.

"It was stronger yesterday, when I saw it first," Dev began. He lifted a skinny finger from the depths of the fur coat. "There is the star we call Jala, and her sister Yima."

Kiria squinted upward. Most of the stars looked the same to her. Haved did the same, tipping backward with one hand on her lower back to steady herself.

"Yima's star has a ghostly image surrounding it." Dev's finger trailed in a tight circle to illustrate. "Jala is cast into shadow. There is a red hue over her now. These things together carry that message, especially when Moktera also appears beside them, but the Hooded One is invisible tonight." The Navigator looked back down at the ground.

I bet it is. Kiria cast a glance at Haved, then back. "Has this message reached the people yet?"

Izal spread his arms in a peaceful gesture. "We have no control over such things. We simply thought it our duty to warn you, since the message held such unfortunate words for your reign. Perhaps there are measures you can take to counteract these prophecies."

This was a sloppy gambit, but a potentially devastating one. Many in the Kingdom thought Kiria had cast it into confusion already, not understanding the part she'd played to save it. The process of spreading the truth was hard enough without adding more lies in the mix.

"Thank you." She nodded at Dev. This poor Navigator had no choice but to do his employer's will, since he provided all his bodily necessities.

Izal bowed his head. "We aim to be helpful."

"I wasn't talking to you," Kiria snapped, finally losing patience. "We both know you made him lie. My people will soon be hungry, despite our storehouses. You can help by continuing to trade with us."

"You understand it is a risk for us," he said, gesturing at Dev, who had taken a step back to stand beside the others.

"Absolutely not," Kiria returned. "The Western Kingdom, the capital in particular, provides the majority of your business. It would be a greater risk for you to step away."

Izal turned to the goateed man at his side as though he were about to whisper something, but then his eyes fell on Haved, and he stayed silent.

"I will not remove the tariffs," she repeated.

"Then, Lady Kiria, there is no way we can justify our continued relationship."

She narrowed her eyes, her pulse thundering. "Who will you trade with, if not with us?"

These weren't ambassadors here in an official capacity, but private businessmen. She couldn't implore them simply based on their position as allies. Only money seemed to have a voice.

Izal looked down the line of his associates breezily enough that it was obvious he was covering some discomfort. "There are many who need what we provide. Charäkhnem itself, for instance."

Kiria realized she was driving her thumbnail into the side of her finger. She wouldn't beg. She was Kiria Arioc and would not be blackmailed.

A chilly breeze drove up from the sea. Dev drew the fur closer around himself. Haved must be getting uncomfortable too, but she had an almost superhuman ability to avoid complaining, which Kiria envied.

Was it worth it to risk severing this tie? There were growers in the south, but would any of them be substantial enough to help get her people through the rest of the year? The consequences of losing this deal could be catastrophic, especially for the poor in her city.

The Western Kingdom was the Charäkhni trader's greatest account. Taking it away would mean ruin for both sides. One of them had to bend, and it wouldn't be her.

"Then we no longer will use your services," she heard herself say, numbness shooting up her back. "You can protect your own reputation against our coming doom"—she couldn't help the sarcasm in her voice—"and I will look elsewhere for a provider. Thank you for coming down. I invite you all to stay another night at the palace before you go on your way. I will personally see you off at midday tomorrow. For now, you are all dismissed. Since you're so cold."

The line of men all gave small bows from the waist. She tried to read their faces, but it was dark and their expressions gave little hint about their reaction. They all kept their eyes on her, fascination glinting there, but not the horror she'd hoped to see.

She forced herself to turn away, knowing they would release the false prophecy to the public and hoping hard that she hadn't made it come true.

***

"I TOLD THEM NO." Exasperated, Kiria raised her arms. "But what if they really do pull away and we have to look somewhere else for food?"

Jori looked at her sideways without moving his head. He sat stock-still on a stool, an artist across the room painting him in profile. From the chest up he looked perfect, his hair falling in waves over his ears, his collar stiff and regal, buttoned to the chin. A crown sat atop his head, gleaming. The part not getting painted wasn't as picturesque. An embroidered sling lay on the ground beside him. To compensate, he had to hold his elbow at a conspicuously uncomfortable angle. He wore no shoes, thick woolen socks (two colors), and his largest pants.

"*Is* there somewhere else? I'm getting thinner as it is. Too many more days with half my regular diet will do me in." His lips twitched an encouraging smile but his eyes betrayed concern swimming below the surface.

"Hopefully."

"Hopefully there are others or hopefully I'll dwindle into nothing?"

Kiria glared good-naturedly. Her own stomach churned with nerves.

"I don't know about these things, darling," he replied. "I wish I could help you but you are the political genius. I'm just supposed to sit here and look pretty. Don't you have Daelon to talk to about this kind of thing?"

"I'm not asking for your advice," she said, although he was right. Daelon's opinion would have been helpful. But she knew what he would say about this. He'd agree with her and pray a little longer in the upper room of the Amiran Academy. "I'm just irritated they would stoop so low."

"It shouldn't surprise you anymore."

"And you're the one I like to vent to."

"I know. Call them horrible names. I won't tell."

The painter glanced up from his work. Maybe he wasn't used to Jori's flippancy yet. In the distance, a hammer clanged.

Kiria squared her shoulders. "I won't call them horrible names." A smile tugged at her lips. "Except in my head."

"That's my girl. Always more diplomatic than I am."

She looked at the light streaming through the window. Nearly midday. "You know you're scheduled to visit the barracks this afternoon, right? To see the soldiers?"

"Yes, yes," he replied.

Jori made these trips every few days, to see to the injured, though there were far fewer of those now than a couple months ago. He remembered all their names and bantered until they felt better.

"I'm meeting with the traders one more time," she said, heading toward the door. "They'd better change their minds." She couldn't very well throw them in her prison without starting an incident between the two countries. The men hadn't broken any laws. They only tried to make money. If Dev spread the lies about her, she might be able to charge them with slander...

"Hopefully they do," he agreed.

"Jori, this means enough food to get everybody through the year."

"Hmm." The noise was genuinely thoughtful. "Have you tried charming them instead of strongarming them?"

"They said I was fated to bring ruin."

"They sound like fun, reasonable people."

Kiria barked a laugh. "I was thinking of inviting them for a friendly game of water ball before they leave. You know, before I bring confusion crashing down on the populace."

"How benevolent."

"My Keeper," sighed the painter, all patience gone, "please stop moving your head."

After a little lift of his brow, Jori crossed his legs and looked obediently forward.

It was time for Kiria to leave anyway. "I'll go," she said, straightening her own metal-and-glass crown.

It was time to see if her risk had paid off.

ONCE AGAIN, a pregnant Haved joined her, but this time they all sat in a meeting room at the far end of the castle. It was warmer here than outside and the sounds of construction were quieter here than in the central section. Several guards stood behind her, as usual, including Royce, the big blond guard who had protected her through the ordeal a few months ago.

Across the table sat the five men in their silks. The Navigator didn't come this time. They only saw him the night before because Kiria had explicitly requested his presence.

After the men remembered themselves upon seeing Kiria again and the usual pleasantries were exchanged—reactions hadn't diminished despite the deep scars on her lip and cheek— Kiria ordered them all coffee. The men seemed grateful. Haved added honey to hers. No one else Kiria had ever met added honey to their coffee, but the servants already knew that she would make a special request and anticipated her now.

All five men passed around the honey when Haved was finished with it. Was this a Charäkhni custom Kiria wasn't aware of?

The man at the end, fat with thick lips and elegant hands, couldn't hide his grimace when he took his first taste. Kiria swallowed a smirk. *Not a custom, then.*

"Tamirat Izal," Kiria began, after taking a delicate sip of coffee, "I'm sorry our working relationship must come to an end."

"I am not sure that it must," he replied.

Kiria's heart pounded once. She steadied herself.

Izal continued. "I'm sure you are full of compassion for your people, Lady Kiria. You have a woman's heart. What are taxes when weighed against the good of your citizens?"

And what are men's hearts? Full of greed? She couldn't keep up this petty inner monologue if she wanted them to acquiesce to what she needed. Instead, she sniffed the bitter sweet steam and turned to Haved, thinking of the honey. "Any leader must care for their people, and we simply cannot afford to lift the tariffs."

Haved stepped in. "There are vast farms in the south that have wanted for many years to trade with the Western Kingdom." Her darkly lined eyes grew sober, almost sad, as she looked at the men. "My Keeper will no doubt utilize those."

At this pronouncement, two of the traders—the one with the trimmed goatee and another who looked a little like a puppy with his huge, baleful eyes—became visibly uncomfortable, shifting in their seats. Kiria's spirits lifted. *Good job, Haved!*

Izal gestured on the table between them with one ringed hand. The largest ring had their business' logo etched on it. "At least we have the satisfaction of knowing that those here in the palace will continue to live in comfort."

He meant it to be polite, but Kiria's throat closed. At least Haved managed a benign look. Kiria, despite the practice she'd had at schooling her features, wasn't sure what kind of expression she wore. It felt like a glare.

"The rations are not only for my people, Tamirat Izal. Did you think we would sit on cushions and eat fruit tarts while our poorest people starve?"

There were smaller traders in the south, but not enough to help all of Brithnem. Maybe if they supplemented with several other companies... It could all be for the best. That way, Kiria wouldn't be beholden to only these few men, but would be better prepared for a future emergency. Regardless of their final decision, she would contact other food suppliers.

Her city would be all right. In time. But first, safety and survival.

She had no more time to waste on these men. "And you," she returned. "I'm sure you won't go hungry atop an excess of food so great that you'll hardly be able to store it all before it rots." She finished her coffee in a decisive sip and stood.

The others stood as well, setting cups in saucers that rattled on the table. Haved still held hers.

"Since we have no more business to conduct," Kiria continued, "let's terminate our time together peaceably. I hope you've enjoyed the hospitality here at Mon Párinath. I'm sorry we could not make you more comfortable. As a gesture of thanks, I hope that you will prevent your Navigator from spreading the... news... that I will bring ruin. My people can find that out for themselves when the time comes, don't you think?" She attempted a smile, but her patience with entitled men had evaporated months ago.

Izal fumbled for words. "Thank you for allowing us to stay, Lady Kiria." He bowed his head first at her, then at Haved. His associates followed suit. "We shall go, then?"

"You're dismissed."

Izal's pink mouth opened in a long, uncertain breath. "What if you reduced the tariffs, Lady Kiria, by half?"

"I've explained my position. I won't continue to argue."

"But—"

"You can accept my terms or leave." She cast a look at the guard Royce, who had already stepped forward meaningfully.

"You strike a hard bargain, My Keeper," Izal said, reaching for levity. The bearded man beside him gave a dry, breathy laugh of support.

Kiria didn't fill the pause.

"We... would be honored to provide our goods to you."

Kiria would not have described Izal's expression as "honored," but a massive sigh of relief flooded her chest at his words.

"We are not heartless," he continued. "Of course your people need food through the winter. Perhaps we can revisit this conversation in the spring."

"We will contact you if we want to revisit it," Kiria said. "I'll have our customs official draw up documents."

Behind her, the door shut as one of the servants left to fetch the official.

Her people wouldn't be hungry this season, and it was because of *her*. She smiled at the businessmen. "My people will escort you out."

More pleasantries and then, mercifully, they were gone. Kiria slumped back down in the chair beside Haved, who continued to hold her cup and take delicate sips. The air seemed fresher, the hammering sounds outside more a sign of new growth than a nuisance.

Kiria beamed. "That was good about the company to the south. I should invite you to these things more often."

Haved's brows twitched in a movement that was half-smile, half-shrug. "I've observed," she said simply. "Well done, My Keeper."

"Kiria, always."

Now Haved really smiled. "Kiria, sister, I will honor you if I like. You have protected your people, so I am not to blame if I address you as Keeper."

"Fair enough," she laughed and squeezed Haved's free hand. "Thank you." Her stomach grumbled in the quiet.

"Lunch is ready," Royce said, carefully intruding on their moment. "I understand that some of the others are already there."

Haved set down her cup and the women stood.

Lunch was half a grilled pear and one large shrimp. The

cook had artfully arranged the small offering with a bright sauce.

"So?" Jori asked after Kiria took her place at the table. He picked up the shrimp by the tail and the meal before him revealed how tiny it was.

"I did it," she said quietly.

Jori's eyes brightened. "You did it?"

"I did it."

"No more rations?"

"No more rations."

"Ha!" Jori jumped up from the table and stuffed the whole shrimp into his mouth at once. In the last few weeks, they'd all learned to eat more slowly so they wouldn't get as hungry throughout the day. "Brilliant. That's my girl. You always were my favorite." He sighed in genuine relief and sat again. "Won't the people be relieved?"

"If they're half as pleased as you, then I'll be happy," she laughed. Her people would know she fought for them, that she'd do her best to take care of them. She glanced at Haved sitting beside her.

A servant approached when she made eye contact. "Yes, My Keeper?"

"One more shrimp for Haved, please. She needs her strength."

No need to feel guilty anymore about their relative comfort in the palace. She'd earned a win, and now they could afford a little celebration to shake off the winter chill. On the horizon, spring was coming.

8

VIKTOR'S STORY

"Ouch!" Viktor cried, clutching his chin and throwing the blade back in the cup on the sink. Blood seeped through his fingers. He hadn't cut himself shaving in months. "Has to be today, doesn't it?" he muttered.

He cleaned himself up with a towel and leaned closer to the glass. The mirror was so low compared to his tall frame that he felt extra gangly every morning as the recruits went through this ritual. He'd only shaved the tattoo-covered side of his face, which didn't show hair as much anyway. The rest of him still looked scraggly.

The others washed their faces and spluttered and joked down the line of sinks, but the din was minimal compared to a normal day. With a crazed sort of laugh, he realized it was because *he* wasn't talking. Viktor's heart had been beating fast for several days now, ever since he heard he would finally get *an appointment*. In his mind, the word was always framed by dramatic pauses. And it should be. An appointment, at last!

Sure, he'd stood at large events, where many guards hemmed in a crowd. But that had been practice. Even if a recruit messed something up, another more experienced guard would be able to pick up the slack. The first time he'd done it—donned the silver armor and seen the three Keepers of the Western Kingdom with his own eyes—he'd burst with pride. He pointed out every face he knew, with facts maybe his friends didn't know, and there were questions, lots of them, along with ways that the guards could be protecting the important dignitaries better and... Afterward, his superior told him he needed to shut up.

Tonight, though, he'd get an appointment. An official one, not just training. He was eighteen, so he was able to handle the full load of a palace guard. The personal guard to one of the Keepers, hopefully.

Why was barracks glass always so streaky and tarnished? He rubbed the little mirror with the side of his fist to take a good look at himself before scraping the blade across his other cheek. One of the other recruits slapped his backside as he was leaving to get him to move out of the way.

"Hey!" Viktor shouted, but he moved. A comeback didn't even occur to him. At least he hadn't cut himself again. He let out a hard breath.

He finished shaving and bent down one last time, staring at his own thin face. Looked good, except for the little cut on his chin. His whole tattoo would stand out against his freshly-shaved skin when they announced where he would serve. The design was a stylized version of a *laird* flower, the lily symbolizing Brithnem, the capital city. He'd gotten it flush across one side of his face, running from jaw to temple.

When he'd first gotten it at fifteen as a declaration of his Khelê heritage, his friends had teased him about becoming an Amir, since some of the most outspoken Khelê ended up studying the Sacred Scroll at the Academy. But he wasn't very interested in that. Honestly, he'd wanted to be a Tanyu when he was a kid. He and his friends would play until it was almost too dark to see and their parents called them inside. The Tanyuin

Academy was the stuff of legends. There were hints about where it might be and what the warriors might do there. The craziest rumors became the loudest because they were the most fun to repeat—warriors on massive green horses with horns on their heads, magic that could make them fly, shapeshifters... It sounded amazing.

Until a few weeks ago.

Viktor ran a hand over his face and stood straight again. He didn't want to think about the news that had come from the Academy, that a whole company had died at the hands of Tanyu. The tragedy meant that several palace guards had rotated out to the army, allowing new recruits to take their places. But Viktor's heart had still broken when he heard.

Instead, since he never received an invitation to join the Tanyuin Academy (a blessing in hindsight) he'd joined the guards-in-training at the palace. He got into the program despite his family being relatively poor citizens with no strong connections to the palace.

He followed the others out of the washroom, and the rest of the morning passed as most others did. Inspections, drills... the usual. Recruits found their voices as the day went on, though tension still settled in a hard knot in Viktor's chest.

Near midday, they were allowed a water break. Most of the young soldiers unfastened their metal breastplates and stood talking in huddles. Sweat plastered Viktor's dark hair to his brow. Armor was a bear to wear in the heat of summer.

"So who do you all hope you get?" he asked the people near him.

The three Keepers, he meant. Most of the recruits hoped for a prestigious position as a guard for one of the royals: Cúron Calthwaite, Kiria Arioc, or Atael Calthwaite.

Everyone spoke at once. All three names jumbled together in

their answers. The mocking looks that followed the dissenting answers made Viktor laugh.

"Don't you all want Cúron?" he asked.

"No!" cried Tanis, a blond recruit a year older than Viktor. "Atael, for sure!"

A chorus of disagreement. Atael had taken over the position as Keeper after his father Aylmor's untimely death a few years ago. The son wasn't as well liked as the father had been.

"Why?" Viktor demanded. "That's a strange choice."

"Why? Because he's never out front at events. He just hangs back all the time. It would be easy to keep an eye on him. Seems like a pushover. Maybe I could even get some ideas across and he could take them to the Main?" Tanis shrugged, keeping one eye on his audience.

"That's true."

"Plus, more free time." The implication made the fellow next to him, Ash, laugh. Ash always fell asleep on night shifts. Irritating. Viktor had thought about ratting him out half a dozen times. Maybe it was a bad reason not to like someone, but a guard ought to take their duties seriously.

"Maybe," Viktor conceded, trying to be charitable. Maybe it wouldn't be so bad to be assigned to Atael. His name didn't bring with it the same prestige as Cúron's did, but prestige wasn't the only reason he'd signed up as a guard-in-training. He loved this kingdom and felt as attached to the Keepers as he was to his own extended family, however problematic the royals sometimes were.

"That's why I'd want Kiria," said Ash.

Disbelieving snorts from several others greeted this declaration. Kiria had recently become the least popular Keeper by far among the three by voicing support of the Tanyu. Viktor felt a little sorry for her, despite not liking her very much.

Last year, when she unveiled that she had Original Beauty,

everyone was intrigued and proud, desperate for the chance to take a look. Viktor's family had danced in the living room as though he'd announced his own marriage engagement instead of a royal's special Ability. And then she'd almost gotten killed and a Tanyu came in the flesh to be her personal bodyguard. People talked about nothing else. Viktor was obsessed with the issue. He learned everything he could about the Tanyu, and about how security could have been better around Kiria before she was attacked by Torithians. The idea that their beloved royal could be in such danger made him even more determined in his drills.

But when she'd returned and taken over the Keepership from her mother, everything fell apart as sure as if she'd cursed the city. The Tanyuin Academy attacked the citizens of Brithnem. People kept dying at random in their sleep. Something the Tanyu were doing caused all the deaths—something about dreams?—but Viktor was helpless to stop it. He'd been afraid to sleep ever since. But Kiria kept defending the Tanyu until the fateful attack, when the Kingdom fought back against the Tanyuin Academy, and all the soldiers who went on that mission were killed. Just like that.

"Why Kiria?" Viktor had agonized over this decision, as though he had some say in who he got to guard. Kiria usually came last on his list.

"You heard about that one time—" Groans drowned out the rest of Tanis' words. He'd told the story a million times. He and Kiria having a stolen moment years ago.

"But, right? Right?" said Ash over the voices. "We already know she likes to..." He made an obscene gesture. "And with guards too! That Tanyu."

At the mention, a few lips flattened in distaste. At least one person here knew someone who'd been killed in the night.

Viktor's dislike of Ash deepened. "That's not how we should

talk about the Keeper," he said. The position itself demanded *some* respect, even if that just meant holding back on the innuendo a little. Good thing no ladies had joined their group. Some, he knew, would have joined right in, but others would have laid Ash out with a punch.

"Ooh!" Ash crooned. "He likes her!"

Viktor huffed. Maybe he would laugh along with his friends if he weren't so stressed. They were idiots sometimes, but they were brave idiots. If it came to it, they'd die in service to any one of the Keepers.

But what if they did assign Viktor to Kiria—currently the most dangerous and controversial position—or didn't attach him to any royal at all? What if he were a door guard in some obscure corner of the palace?

"No," he said. "I would want Lord Cúron because he believes in Khelê causes. I think it would be an honor, and I know—I know!—you all think I talk too much about the Khelê. Probably you do. It doesn't matter. Cúron thinks about us, so I think that would be best." Secretly, he suspected that Cúron's personal guards got a little extra coin as well, which he'd be able to send to his family as a happy surprise.

"You wouldn't get Cúron!" said Ash. "No one would be able to see him around you."

"And you're terrible in the races," Tanis joined in. Sometimes guards and servants held unofficial races on the beach behind the palace.

"Hey, I'm pretty good!" Viktor protested. He'd raced just last week but he was off his usual pace because of the bad news he'd just gotten about the lost company of soldiers. It had been a bad week. No need to judge him on that one performance. He absently stroked the cut on his chin.

"I pick Cúron too," struck in a new voice. It was Viktor's friend Kenno, who proceeded to curse at the rest of the group on

Viktor's behalf. "He's the best one. We all know it."

Kenno looked older than his eighteen years, with a full beard and pale skin.

"Okay, okay," said Ash. "Who gets who?"

Tanis leaned back against the barracks wall in a self-satisfied way and pointed to each of them in turn. "Cúron, Atael, Kiria." Kenno, Ash, Viktor.

Viktor stepped forward. "I don't think that's—"

Their commander called for the end of the water break.

⎯⎯⎯⎯⎯⎯

AFTER MORE DRILLS and extra cleaning to prepare for assignments, the recruits got a few hours off before appointment time. Most people spent the hours seeing family or significant others since they would effectively be living at the palace even more so going forward. Viktor went home to see his parents and sister in the poorer neighborhood of Farmers Guard.

The kitchen at home smelled like fresh fish and savory broth. The mess hall at the barracks never smelled this good. Faintly, Viktor heard the bubbling of the stew in the pot on the adjacent counter. White fish, just for him. He sliced the leafy top off the fennel, letting it fall on the chopping board, then he took the rest of the meaty part in bite-sized sections.

Tinny chimes sounded in another room. Probably his sister Luna with another one of her projects. Every time he saw her, she changed, growing stranger and stranger, but in the best way. She was fourteen now, gangly, like him, but blonde and obsessed with inventions. Not blonde right now—she'd used beet juice to dye her hair pink. She wasn't asked to help with dinner because, as his mother explained, "It will be too many people."

She used the old tongue to say it. In Viktor's household, his parents would sometimes slip into the old tongue instead of the common one. Many generations of Khelê heritage had preserved the language that nobody spoke as their first anymore.

Viktor looked down at the vegetable he was chopping. The knife went up and down, slicing through the flesh to create thin disks that fell in neat rows. The exercise calmed him.

"Ack, Viktor!" cried his mother, hustling over to him from where she stood at the stewpot.

She came only to his sternum, but he stepped back and presented the fennel.

"That's not how you do it." Her criticism turned to laughter, even as she took the knife from him with her three-fingered hand and shoved him away with her hip. "These pieces are wrong for the meal." She looked up at him with a twinkle in her eye. "I should have known when you were not speaking like a follow string."

"That is the oldest saying you could possibly use," he shot back playfully in the common tongue, daring to come a little closer to see if he really had messed up the fennel. The round, flat disks probably wouldn't go well in his celebratory stew. But didn't they have sauce they could put on them instead?

"A follow string?" said his mother, creasing her black eyebrows. "I suppose I hadn't thought about what it means. It must be a string that guides you through a maze or something. It keeps going and going and going..." She smiled. "I'll take over," she said, returning to the common tongue. "You get your sister. Dinner will be ready in a few minutes."

"And you said there would be loquat cake for after?" Just the thought of it made Viktor's mouth water.

His mother gestured to a bowl on the counter, evidence that she had already started making the dessert.

They smiled at each other. His mother's smile. He only saw it every couple weeks. That wasn't enough. "All right, but I want half that cake for myself," he said.

"Half? That's an enormous amount."

"I'm a growing boy."

"I hope not. You're a giant."

Viktor was unusually tall, but then everyone in his family was unusual. A consequence of being proudly Khelê. "I hope I grow twice as tall," he said. "Then I could have all the loquat cake instead of half."

His mother made a dismissive noise as Viktor turned to find Luna. The tinny noise got louder down the hall with the bedrooms. He knocked on Luna's door. "It's me," he called. When they were both children, she'd made it clear that he wasn't just to walk in. If he did, she'd fly into a brief but horrifying rage.

"Come in." She had a low and husky voice for a young girl. It made her sound travel-tired.

When he entered, Luna hunched on the floor over a wooden contraption with a small circular handle, moveable dowels, and shallow metal cups.

"I can't get it to sound right," she said, lifting her head to look at him. "Listen." She turned the handle and the shafts of wood lifted up and down in a pattern that beat against the metal dishes. A quiet but clearly out-of-tune cacophony resulted. When the song finished, Luna sat back and crossed her legs in resigned thought, her brow screwed tight.

"That's pretty neat to me," said Viktor, crouching to take a closer look. "Mother said dinner will be ready soon."

Luna gave a dismissive gesture with her bone-thin wrist. The machine still obviously dominated her thoughts. She was hard to deal with like this.

"It's seafood stew and loquat cake," Viktor went on, "in honor of me—of my official appointment later tonight. They're going to choose where I'll be stationed, for which Keeper. We were talking about who would be the best, but I don't know for sure. Lord Cúron, right? That's what Father would say."

"Do you want to work for Cúron?" Luna asked. "Are you good enough?"

Viktor straightened and puffed out his chest. "Of course I am! I've been doing guard duty for years now. You know that. I know all the royals."

"You've *seen* all the royals." Luna finally turned her scrutinizing attention fully to Viktor. Her eyes were glass green and, despite being thin like him, her features were more crowded to the center of her little face, punctuated by a slightly snubbed nose. It was as though her face had frozen into a scheming expression, perfect for her inventions or for sussing him out.

"I've seen them, and I've met them too," he said. "I want Lord Cúron."

"Well, you obviously don't want Lady Kiria, do you?"

"I guess not."

"You guess not?" she exclaimed, quickly giving her eyes a roll. "Such a boy."

He flushed. "No. I mean, yes, but I just mean that that's not what I meant."

"Calm down. Nobody wants Lady Kiria, so I bet that's who you get." Her smile turned impish. "Bet a token?"

They weren't supposed to bet, but Viktor gambled on the beach races all the time. He fished in his trousers and took out two battered tokens. On them was stamped a younger version of Cúron's bearded face in profile. "Two!"

"What's the bet?"

"I think I'll get Lord Cúron, and you think I'll get somebody else."

"Odds are better my way. I win if you get Lord Atael too."

"Well," said Viktor obstinately, dropping the tokens back in his pocket, "I'm sure I'll get Cúron."

"You weren't sure a minute ago."

"I'm sure now. I'm—"

Their mother's voice rose above their argument. "Dinner!"

Luna cranked the handle of the little machine one last time. "I'll have to adjust the depth," she muttered, flicking one of the metal dishes before standing. She tucked her pink hair behind both ears and went out of the room with Viktor.

The stew smelled thick and heavenly. Father had joined Mother in the kitchen. His face was a mottled red and white in uneven patches. He had gotten his Khelê tattoo to cover his shoulder and trace the natural patterns of his face. It was an unusual design, much more unusual than Viktor's *laird* flower. Now the white patches on his cheeks were redder than usual with exertion.

"What was that I was hearing as I packed up?" he asked Luna, handing her a ladled bowl of stew.

"Music machine," she answered.

He handed a bowl to Viktor next. Flat disks of fennel floated at the top.

Viktor tried to push them down with the back of his spoon, but they bobbed right back up. "It doesn't sound very good, but it looks like an interesting design so she'll probably figure it out. Did you say packing?"

"Packing for the trip. The three of us have to go visit your mother's aunt in Skirwith. She's not doing well these days, so we'll be there for the whole winter. At least we'll get to hear about your appointment before we leave, eh?"

Luna set down her bowl of stew on the table and put her hands on her hips. "He's getting Lady Kiria," she said.

Father sank in a chair with his dinner, looking slightly stricken. "That's not true, is it?"

Mother put a hand on his upper arm and sat beside him. "They haven't decided appointments yet."

"It would be an honor to serve any of the Keepers," Viktor found himself saying, although his mouth had gone dry. Nerves, now that the actual decision was coming near, jumped around in his chest. He hadn't thought much about how his parents would have strong opinions.

"I bet him he won't get Cúron," said Luna, dipping into her bowl for a piece of white fish.

His mother smacked Viktor's arm. "You didn't! You bet again?"

"Just two tokens."

"Keep the two tokens. Keep the two tokens," said Father, now soothing his wife. "Of course he'll get whatever appointment he wants."

The conversation veered toward his mother's aunt.

Viktor stared at the pieces of fennel in the stew, pressed them down again. He waited a few seconds for his stomach to settle before taking the first bite.

LIGHTS from the palace glowed faintly even out to the barracks. Across the main training field stood the dome of the Amiran Academy, with its round lanterns that were never put out. Quietly, waves splashed in the distance.

All the recruits standing in two lines were uncharacteristically quiet, even more so than they'd been that morning. The dark air felt like a held breath. Words rose up to choke Viktor but he managed to swallow most of them.

"Did you see your family today?" he whispered to Kenno.

His friend angled his face only slightly. "I went out with friends. Girlfriend."

"Oh, that's great. How is she? You're talking about Lancerel, right? I mean, of course you are. I haven't seen her since—"

"Viktor." Kenno stood stiffly at attention to demonstrate what Viktor should be doing besides jabbing.

Viktor held back a sigh. Talking helped tame the fluttering in his stomach.

Maybe it was good that Luna and his parents were going to Skirwith for a while. If he didn't get Cúron, the sting would have worn off by the time they came back. He slipped his hand in his pocket and rubbed the two tokens together.

"The duty of service is noble," he muttered to himself in the old tongue. His father had said that right after he had been accepted as a recruit. Viktor didn't speak the old language much, but it seemed to fade into the darkness more than saying something intelligible to everybody. And he had to talk to calm his nerves.

Official appointments weren't particularly ceremonious beyond a simple announcement. Everyone lined up. Names and appointments were read. Everyone went back to their room in the barracks to sleep, unless they got a night shift. Simple, but, for a while anyway, life-changing.

Cúron. Cúron, please.

His parents would be so proud, and Luna would owe him two tokens. He found himself humming the dreadfully nonsensical tune that her machine had made. By the time he saw her again, it would be flawless. That's just how she was.

"Shut up," Kenno breathed.

Viktor stopped humming. He took his hand out of his pocket.

Lanthe, one of the commanders, stepped forward in her full armor, white skin glowing. She held a piece of paper. Behind her stood a man holding a lantern so she could read. "Tanis Restino," came her strong voice, "Atael Calthwaite, center exterior door to Third Keeper's wing. Report midday. Una Withly, Cúron Calthwaite, bedchamber door, report sunrise."

That was the shift Viktor wanted. The day shift guarding Cúron. Was there another appointment that good?

Lanthe ran through several more names. One guarded Atael's bedchamber at night, another Kiria's Second Keeper hallway, and yet another was alternate door guard for the Main, which was the huge space where all three met to discuss policy. He hadn't even considered that one.

"Viktor," Lanthe called. Khelê had no last names.

His heart seized. A little sound emerged from his throat. He cleared it to cover up the panicked noise. "Yes?" he said, before remembering that no one else had responded to their name. The darkness hid his flush, but couldn't hide his discomfort. He was too tall, and the slight shift in his weight, back and forth, when he was supposed to stand stock-still, showed like wind through the trees.

"Kiria Arioc, safe house, report immediately."

His whole body drooped. Kiria? The safe house? That was far from the palace, outside the walls in a patch of woody area in the main city. And... the night shift? This couldn't have gone any worse. He wouldn't so much as *see* Cúron to help him if there were trouble. Or Kiria, for that matter. He couldn't help anyone, as he longed to do. What were the chances that Kiria would need to use the emergency safe house? Yet now he had to guard it all night long.

His legs felt heavy when the recruits were dismissed. Kenno, who had gotten an appointment guarding Cúron's son, cast him an apologetic glance in the low light. Viktor didn't say anything. He just went inside to pick up the seeds that would help him stay awake all night, and trudged out toward the far and hidden safe house, thinking of the tokens in his pocket.

9

———

MASTER TANERY

Bard was the only one.

He was the only one in his family to receive an invitation to the Tanyuin Academy, the only Tanyuin advisor in the royal court, the only advisor who was not already given full religious training as an Amir, and the only soon-to-be Amir who was romantically attached. With every step, he felt like he was doing something wrong, because there was no one to tell him how this life should go.

Well, not every step. He was just stressed. *Only stress.*

Morning light, barely gray, seeped into the room where he lay under the covers. He closed his eyes, blocking out the view of the intricately molded ceiling. *Grant us to live in love and not in hatred, in action instead of apathy, to display the will of God in a spirit of humility and hope, sacrificing, by your light, all that stands—*

Lips touched his forehead in a kiss.

Bard's eyes flew open. Jori flopped back down beside him on the bed as though he'd been caught doing something wrong. "I thought you were asleep," he said, his unapologetic tone not matching his body language.

"I was muttering to myself."

"You do that all the time. Every night. You can see how I'd get confused." Jori's hair looked almost as wild as Bard's always did, the brown waves bending every which way. A smirk twisted his mouth.

Bard sighed. "How often do you wake up before me? Especially today, yeah?"

"Had to take advantage of the rare opportunity." Jori's gray eyes flashed impishly as he angled up on his elbow, but there was the slightest undercurrent of question in them too. Unsurprisingly, the question came out right away. "Not too much?"

That was another way that Bard was a rare species, maybe the only one. He'd never met another, anyway. He liked Jori. A lot. In fact, he loved Jori, but he'd never looked at him *that way*, not like Firian and Kiria looked at each other, with their wedding days away. Maybe he never would have realized how much he liked Jori if the Keeper hadn't made the first move. It would have been friendship forever. When Bard told him the truth, early on, with a burning face and eyes boring into the rug at his feet, Jori had laughed and gestured at himself and said, "How could you resist this?" But Bard was serious. He'd never been interested in more than talking and laughing and cuddling. It turned out he liked kissing too, to Jori's delight. Still, years later, they were figuring out a comfortable compromise. But even with all his other options as the most charismatic Keeper of the Western Kingdom, Jori had stayed.

"You know it's not too much," Bard answered, smiling and giving him a quick hug before jumping out of bed. "Just make sure I'm awake next time, yeah?"

Jori groaned. "Already? We already have to wake up?"

"I do," he said, pulling on a linen shirt and casting around to find his Amiran robe. "You don't." Did he send it out to be washed for today?

*—sacrificing, by your light, all that stands in hindrance to our…
our what?*

He gnawed his lip, anxiety rising. That was one of the passages from the Sacred Scroll that he wasn't sure he could recite if Herne Gautham asked. Distractedly, he opened the curtains.

"Ah, you plan to murder me!"

Bard ignored Jori's dramatics. "*All that stands in hindrance… And sacrificing, by your light, all that stands in hindrance to your…*" The words jumbled, refusing to stand in line. So many of the passages from the Scroll fell neatly into place after he figured out the cadence, or the meaning, or connected one word to the next like moves in a game. Not that this was a game. Far from it. But words were like puzzle pieces once he focused them into place. It was easier than Master Gerand's *katah* class, when he had once had to stare at a seashell for half the afternoon without moving, and another time had spent all day building geometric shapes to learn was focus truly meant, all to hone him into a weapon to kill. This—studying the Sacred Scroll to serve the thrones of Brithnem—was actually fulfilling. He'd thought it would be like a class, but there was more. Early mornings and late nights squinting into candlelit texts, probing questions given and taken, a language learned, prayers lifted, awe at the supernatural around him, and a sense of being exactly where he belonged, even if he did go to bed exhausted every night.

And all that training would end today. If he passed.

"*Grant us to live in love and not in hatred…*"

"How many people," said Jori, swinging into view around him, "have managed to learn all this stuff in only four years, hm? Darling, you'll be wonderful."

"But—"

"Look." Jori pointed at Bard's hand. He still wore the Master ring he'd earned at the Academy. It glinted black on his finger.

When Bard looked back up, Jori met his gaze and let a meaningful silence stretch out to make his point for him. Scratching his nose delicately, he concluded, "*Nobody* is as good as you."

Bard felt heat rise in his cheeks and he smiled. "You haven't seen the robe, have you, mate?"

"Of course. You need it for official days. I'd never let it get lost."

Bard doubted that.

Jori must have seen the skepticism on his face, because he opened a wardrobe and pulled the high-collared, blue-gray robe of the Amir off a hook in the back. He raised an eyebrow as though he'd scored a point.

"I should never question you."

Jori grinning, helping Bard ease his paralyzed hand into the sleeve. "You're learning."

The robe fell as long as a Tanyuin coat, all the way to his ankles. Bard watched his own reflection in the glass as though he were looking at somebody else. His image, with its wild black hair, crooked nose, and hooked fingers, didn't match his vision of an Amir. But what was an Amir, really? They were noted for their diversity, given that so many Khelê volunteered for the training. His uniqueness wouldn't stand out. It told his story.

Jori, a second wave of bleariness making his movements a little messy, started fastening the buttons up the front of the robe. A swiftly fading smile of gratitude crossed Bard's face.

If he passed his test today, Bard would officially be an Amir as well as a Tanyu. It would mean a landmark moment for Kiria, the First Keeper, who had made a project out of painstakingly bringing the two Academies closer together as allies. It would mean having true legitimacy in the eyes of the Kingdom as Jori's advisor. And it would mean he could help officiate the wedding.

Tests before this one had been for himself, maybe for the

honor of his family, but passing this test meant more than any since the Autumn War.

———

HERNE SCRATCHED HIS WHITE BEARD. The color stood out sharply against his darkly tanned skin. At the first sound of his familiar, lilting voice, Bard had felt at home with the old man. When Bard first started his lessons four years ago, Kiria had requested Herne for him since he was the only Amir from Enderin.

In a way that reminded Bard of the docks back home, full and rasping, Herne said, "There's no more study for today."

Bard sat forward. The space was cramped, little more than a cell with enough space for two people and the sacred book perched on a stand. He knit his brows. "No more practice?"

"Do you need more?"

"I..."

"I don't think you need more. No one studies the day of the test."

Bard doubted that, but he rarely spent any time with other students, since any time he wasn't here, he was busy working for Jori and Kiria. Plus, he was older than all of the others, most of whom were still teenagers.

"No one does. Least of all a busy advisor." Herne's black eyes twinkled.

Bard managed half a smile. "You think I've done enough?"

"You will keep learning through your life."

The answer wasn't an answer. "If there's something else I can do, I don't mind."

"Relax. Pray. The examination isn't a test like the others only to determine your knowledge of the Scroll. It's to see if you are ready to be an Amir, yeah?"

A real smile tugged at Bard's features. Herne sounded so

Endrian. "Okay."

"This place is stuffy," said Herne, stretching in his small seat. Usually, he could sit still far longer than Bard, who always wanted to rattle his leg or tap his finger to let out energy. "Let's go out. I'll order tea."

"Well, that sounds nice, but—"

"But what? But nothing!" He dismissed the thought with a sweep of his weathered hand. Standing, he opened the door.

The space was so small that Bard had to move his chair to let Herne pass. A knowing smile played on the old man's features as he stepped into the light. Bard followed.

The sunlight burned his eyes. As much as he wanted tea, and he did—good, strong tea with heavy dregs and sugar—his nerves rebelled against the idea. With the test so close, was it right to relax with his mentor instead of doing all he could to prepare?

Herne walked at a deliberate pace to a round table sitting on the patio behind the palace. His breath came in a heavy breath as he sat. Bard placed himself opposite. Distractedly, he pressed his fingertip into the metal edge of the tabletop.

"An Amir is what?" Herne asked, returning Bard to the moment at hand.

"Holy, studious, devoted, wise," he recited.

The first one had intimidated him at first, when he heard the list. He'd wanted to shrink into the floor. Holy? How could he be holy, especially after all he'd done? Still, the Torithian captain appeared in his dreams, debauched and horrible, but alive, until Bard ripped his life away. And then the people who lost their lives taking the city tof Brithnem back for its rightful owners. Everyone had known the risks, but he was the one who spear-headed the planning. Any oversight or weak spot fell on him.

That first day, so much of the confidence built up in him had crumbled like cake. Jori had hugged him and spoken reassuring things in his ear, painting himself out to be far worse, yet in a higher position of authority, so Bard shouldn't feel bad at all. Everyone was terrible. Later, the Scroll had taught Bard more, and hope had replaced his feelings of insufficiency. *Forgive one another and turn from your ways. Lift your heads and you will be washed clean.* It was one of the first passages he memorized. Ever since, it had stuck with him. Jori knew that one too. It was near his favorite section, the one that included the line he'd chosen for his royal tattoo: *May it rain hope always.*

Bard still didn't feel holy, but he strove to be all those things. Sometimes he tipped his head up to feel the sun or the rain on his face.

"Holy, studious, devoted, wise," Herne repeated. "And thirsty. We Endrians need our tea. Kingdom folks don't understand how to do it right."

"No, they don't." Bard smiled, despite himself.

Herne pinched the fabric of his robe at the throat as though it could close more tightly. "I'm glad we see eye to eye." He lowered his head. "Bard, my son, you know the Scroll, and there's nothing more today that you can do to sway the minds of the council. Allow yourself a moment's peace, yeah? Besides," Herne coughed, "I don't feel up to teaching more today."

Bard flattened his lips in obvious indecision, but the Amir once again shooed away Bard's fearful thoughts. He had to admit, it was more enjoyable to sip tea in a sunlit garden with a man he'd come to see as family than to practice rapid-fire questions.

The cups came and they sat together in amicable silence.

FOUR AMIR SAT in the formal dining room next to the Main. All wore high-collared robes and serious expressions. Bard stood before them on the opposite side of the long table. He swallowed against his dry throat.

The day had passed too quickly. He should have played Indisfate with Kiria or run with Firian on the beach, if he weren't occupied with his duties as a bodyguard. Maybe they could have found a way to eat lunch together. Something. Instead, he'd studied all day, ironing out the passages in his mind. Too much rode on this test. He had to pass.

One of the Amir had something on his nose. It might have been a small mole, but for some reason, Bard couldn't stop staring at it. Amusement twisted Daelon's features slightly. He must have noticed. *Holy, yeah?*

"How many hours a day have you dedicated to the work of God?" asked the man with the mole who sat next to Daelon.

"The... studying?"

"The work of God," Daelon repeated, nodding with encouragement.

"All of them."

"In your opinion, how should the royal household grow?"

Chetana had given him an idea that this question was coming. He opened his mouth to answer.

"Did you pray for guidance?"

Bard nodded quickly. He'd spent time in the holy place in the upper floor of the Amiran Academy, but as this test got closer, he spent less time there. There was so much to know that there hadn't been time.

Questions cycled through, one after the other. Bard chanted the Scroll, answered questions... As the test went on, the people in front of him seemed to shrink. They'd grown in his imagination until they blocked his path forward. Now they were friends. He had endured so, so much more. Why had he feared this test at all?

By the end of the interview, he felt buoyant, barely touching the ground as he returned to his room. Because of the importance of the Amir's decision, which they would deliver later that night, no other duties were assigned to him. A very rare day off.

Could a Tanyu become an Amir after all? His Tanyuin training would always be with him, but maybe he could have this too. It seemed like too much.

He couldn't wait to tell Jori. But Jori wasn't there.

After asking the guards, who were reasonably sure Jori had gone for a walk after a diplomatic lunch, Bard headed to the beach. Five figures dotted the private stretch of sand behind the palace. Three guards and, at the center, Jori and Kiria. Apparently, Kiria had convinced Jori to fly kites, not that it would take much convincing. Despite being in his mid-twenties, Jori could never resist something like this.

Kiria held the string and Jori kept throwing the kite Bard had helped him put together more than a year ago, but it didn't stay aloft. Endrians flew kites during certain festivals, but it wasn't as though Bard had made them himself as a child before he was brought to the Tanyuin Academy. Still, they did their best. The yellow kite *looked* right, at least.

"Run," Jori said, words faint with distance.

Kiria obeyed, running along the sand, looking backward at the bumbling kite.

Bard walked slowly, content to watch for a while, before he stood next to Firian, keeping watch as Kiria's bodyguard. No wonder he'd felt that Firian was out here.

His friend's dark eyebrow rose at the sight of Bard in the Amiran coat, and a small smirk spread over his face. "So it's that day?" Firian asked. As usual, he wore the black pants and shirt of the Tanyuin Academy. No jacket today. It was warm outside.

Bard ran his finger along the inside of his high collar. "Yeah." Then he beamed. "I think I'm going to get it, going to pass the test. I did really well."

"You recited the entire Scroll this morning?" Firian was only partly teasing.

"No, there's more than that, but—"

Jori's running feet crunching along the sand cut off his words. "I see that smile, darling. Did you amaze them all with your knowledge and general greatness?"

"I think so, yeah."

Jori hugged him sideways and kissed the side of his head loudly. "Marvelous. If they hadn't recognized how hard you worked and how adorable and indispensable and brilliant you are, then I would have had to use my full Keeper power on them. No more Amiran Academy."

"Enough jokes, Jori," Kiria put in, approaching with the kite in her hand.

"It's not official," Bard said.

"But you'll get it." Jori's flushed face and bright eyes really did look proud.

"I hope so." He tried to stifle a grin, but it came out anyway.

"When do you find out?" Kiria asked, handing Jori the yellow kite. "It's defective, I think."

"Maybe you weren't running fast enough."

"It's harder in a dress. I'll wear pants next time and then you'll see." Kiria shared a look with Firian. Warmth sparked between them.

"They'll tell me as soon as they've decided," Bard said, a tiny pang of apprehension creeping in again. If he was wrong, then he couldn't help with the wedding, which was only four days off.

Just then, Amir Daelon, Kiria's advisor, strolled down to the beach. He didn't make a habit of frequenting the water, preferring to stay inside to study undisturbed, so he had to be coming to tell Bard the news. His gut seized with second guesses. Jori fished for his hand and squeezed it reassuringly. Slightly calmer, Bard squeezed back.

"My Keepers," Daelon greeted, bowing from the waist when he reached the edge of the grassy embankment overlooking the sand. "Master Tanery." His attention swiveled to Bard. There they stood in those matching outfits, Bard's pulse pounding. "I'm afraid Amir Gautham has fallen suddenly ill. He's asking for you."

Jori's hand tensed, and Bard frowned deeply, nearly dizzy with undermined anticipation. "What?"

"He's had an episode. I think you should come now."

"Is he... all right? Will he be okay?" Herne was a hale man, despite his age. He wasn't prone to "episodes," at least not that Bard was aware of.

Daelon pursed his lips. "I don't know. His request was for you."

A rock settled in Bard's throat. He felt the attention of the others staring at him like sunshine heat, oppressive. A line of sweat beaded on his neck and ran down his back. "Okay." His mouth was dry.

He numbly walked away from the others to follow Daelon.

"I'll check on you later," said Jori's voice.

"We will," Kiria echoed.

It was a short walk to the Amiran Academy, but Daelon walked past it to the barracks, passing through a side door into what looked like a medical ward. Beds were lined up against the walls. Small tables beside each held jars and bandages and, in some cases, blades. The smell was herbal and sharp. A strong memory burst over him of a dark room and pain in his spine as it bent backward. Or maybe that was later. Dreamlike medicine. Firian jogging awkwardly with him as though they ran in a three-legged race.

He ran his good hand over the one frozen halfway into a fist. Focusing again on the room, he scanned for Herne. One doctor tended to a woman groaning in pain in the far corner. Three of the beds were occupied, not in a row but far away from one another. The one closest to the door held a white-bearded man. Bard hurried to him.

"Have you heard whether you passed? I know... you were concerned," the Amir asked through labored breaths as Bard knelt beside the bed. Nothing outwardly seemed wrong with him. No blood. Just some tiredness in Herne's normally sharp eyes. A month ago he had pointed out a songbird, bright green and barely visible in the foliage. Bard had already forgotten what it was called.

"No. But it doesn't matter," Bard said quickly. "Daelon said you wanted me."

Daelon stood back a few paces to give them privacy, but the doctor approached.

"I did," said Herne.

Bard lifted his eyes to the doctor, now standing above them. "He'll be all right, yeah? When will he get out?"

The doctor's face grew more lined. "We're just making him comfortable," he replied.

It wasn't hard to figure out that code. Bard rubbed his stubbled chin and the back of his head rapidly, trying to understand it all. Just this morning Herne was fine.

A hand touched his arm, bringing him back to reality. "It's all right," said the Amir, his voice still strong. "I'm not afraid, but I wanted to make sure I saw you first."

Bard would miss that voice. *Don't think that way.* "No, I'm sure there's something we can do. Um... some medicine or treatment or something. Prayer!" He bowed his head, clearing his mind as though he were going into the Unreal. *Reverence, submission...*

Bard peeked up to find Herne giving him a knowing smile. "God doesn't only bend to you. Sometimes you must bend to him."

Bard gnawed the inside of his lip. It was too soon. Curving his mouth downward, he said, "I don't—"

"You won't become an Amir this time." Herne said it decisively, without malice.

Bard nearly sputtered. "Why? Why not?"

"You are too divided. An Amir must be single-minded in devotion."

"I've worked really hard!" He didn't mean to be arguing with the old man, but surely he must be wrong, right?

The man chuckled. "You have. You have. And your heart is pure. It just has many concerns. You can still serve the Kingdom with your knowledge."

But... He didn't know where to begin a counterargument. His status wasn't even decided yet, but he felt as though he'd received an iron-bound verdict. *I could do... more...* But he couldn't. He had friends and family and politics. He was the liaison between Amir and Tanyu. He was Firian's point person when he went on mission. He was Jori's advisor. He studied late into the night, chewing seeds to help him stay awake.

He didn't have more to give.

"What do I do?" he asked softly.

"Keep going," Herne replied. "You're young."

Not as young as the other Amir in training... His twenty-three years felt as heavy as forty.

"This won't be the only time you can take the test."

Bard swallowed thickly. All his legitimacy, for himself, for Kiria, for Firian, for Jori—gone. "What about the wedding?"

Knowledge of his own selfishness nearly sent him rocketing to his feet. Herne was... dying... and Bard was talking about himself. "I'm sorry, I'm sorry. Is there anything you'd like me to say for you? What was the real reason you wanted to see me?"

"There's nothing wrong with the friendly face of home, yeah?"

"Yeah." *Accept it.* But he wanted to run to the Holy Place now and beg for Herne's life, not just wait for him to breathe his last. "Jori and Kiria are flying kites on the beach."

"Kites!"

Bard beamed, though he felt his eyes getting red. "Bad day for it, though. Not enough wind."

Herne held up a finger. "Or not running fast enough." His eyes grew dreamy with memory.

"I'll let you rest," Bard said, patting the corner of the sickbed as he turned to go.

"Bard."

"Hm?"

"It'll be all right."

Bard could only nod in return.

It wasn't as though he hadn't seen death, but he didn't want to see another. More, now that the Kingdom had relative peace, felt unfair.

Hours later, he found himself staring at the blue and gold ceiling of the Holy Place, empty of prayers. He didn't know what to say anymore.

That was where the Amir found him to give him the news. Herne was right. He didn't pass the test. Something about mindset, they said. Bard stayed until it got dark. Students cycled in and out. He flipped through pages of the Scroll, pain hollowing inside him.

Finally, he returned to the palace. Disappointment and grief battled inside him, thick and heavy. When he returned to his room, Jori practically flew at him. For once, he didn't say anything, just crushed Bard in a hug. Bard buried his face in his shoulder.

"I'm sorry," he murmured.

"For what?" Jori asked.

"For not becoming a full Amir. It would have been so good for your—"

"Oh, shut up. I'm just glad you aren't dead somewhere. When you didn't come back, I pictured many horrible things. What could keep you away from *us*?"

Bard backed out of the hug. "Herne is... Amir Gautham... He's not all right."

Jori's eyes turned sympathetic. "What a day you've had! My, my... Calls for a drink."

"I don't want one."

"Of course you do." Jori swiveled on his toes and opened a cabinet by the dresser. With one hand he pulled out a pair of long-stemmed glasses, and with the other, some sparkling wine. "I need you to sit down with me and tell me everything, and I will tell you how much you are not a disappointment and comfort you about Herne." He clinked one glass at a time on the vanity, filling them up without spilling either. He looked like a magician.

Despite himself, Bard's insides loosened. He took the wine and sipped. It was bubbly and cool.

Jori leaned closer. "I chose you for my advisor before you'd ever taken Amir lessons."

Bard bunched his mouth to the side. "The wedding's in four days," he said quietly.

"And what are they going to say? 'Well, Bard failed completely so we can't let him near our wedding. It's not like he saved all our lives or anything.'"

Herne's words came back to him. *It'll be all right.* With his mentor teetering on the edge of death, it was hard to be so cavalier. The high neck of the Amiran robe felt starchy against his throat, all the buttons a daunting barrier.

"I prayed for him," Bard said after a pause.

"Firian? God knows he needs it."

"No, Herne. But I think... I think he's still going to..."

Jori threw back the rest of his drink so he could set the glass down and hold Bard again, who felt tears welling in his eyes. "Shhh. I'm still here. Kiria too, and Firian. There's the ocean and fireflies and kites and songs and cinnamon toast." Bard felt Jori's words against his ear. "There's your horrible grainy tea and an insufferable Charäkhni ambassador here for the wedding that I had to entertain all morning with my brilliant conversation. Life, my dear, is still good."

Jori took Bard's face in his hands and kissed him. "It'll be all right."

HERNE DIED TWO DAYS LATER.

Bard would still be one of the three Amir under the canopy during the wedding, which made him glad, but didn't completely take away the sting of failing the test. *Too divided.* He'd tried not to be. To be an Amir and a Tanyu were maybe mutually exclusive, the result of wholehearted pursuits. Then what was Bard? The only one trying to fully understand both Academies from the inside.

Bard adjusted his grip on the pole he held, gauzy material swinging. Like the others on the dais with him, he wore the high-necked coat of an Amir, but he'd requested the tailor to make his a darker shade.

Whatever he was, Tanyu was part of it.

Huge arrangements of blue and purple *laird* flowers transformed the area around the dais until it looked like a garden rather than the familiar Main. Chains of flowers even hung from the ceiling in long, clustering strands. The fragrance permeated the room. From his spot on the dais, Bard could see the mosaic of the four royal Lines inlaid in the floor, now like an opulent outdoor patio.

A light blue runner, silky as water, ran from the dais steps to the double doors at the side of the Main where the couple would enter. Chairs sat in a thick semi-circle nearby. Along the walls soared the huge statues of the founders and below them, guards at attention, as well as a small group of musicians and tables laden with food and drink. An enormous fruit tart rose three tiers on a series of wide platters.

Finally, his gaze ascended skyward, tracing up the multi-paned windows to the words—still slightly smudged with smoke—that ran along the joint of the high ceiling.

In whatever you do, worship Him.

Shifting light filtered over Daelon's pale face as he held the pole opposite Bard. Slanting through the fabric, it danced across Chetana's darker one as though the shadows were a living thing, playing in the sunlight. The sense, once again, of an outdoor space—a garden or grotto—took Bard again. Something loosened in his chest as guests began to arrive and the music played. Faraway anticipation, searing delight, beat against his chest as though it were struggling to get free. Bard only felt parts of it, like being warmed by smoke when the wind turned. Firian waited behind the side doors, unintentionally charging Bard with his excitement.

There was Commander Lanthe, who stood her ground against Master Belik during the Autumn War. There was Master Erron, now the Head of the Tanyuin Academy, and, long ago, the Hall Master overseeing the row that included the small room Bard had shared with Firian. Mayor Blackwater of Rantoul stood a little distance from Charäkhni dignitaries. A stately couple with more modest dress entered. His bearing declared him to be a soldier, though not one Bard had seen before, yet the man wasn't the one who held his attention. The woman, perhaps in her mid-twenties, had long, glossy dark hair, fair skin, and serious blue eyes that Bard knew well. Firian's sister, Brett.

Bard grinned. He'd have to introduce himself to her. They saw each other a few years before, briefly, when Firian's family came to the Academy, but they hadn't spoken. And that man must be her husband. It was high time they all knew each other.

A musical flourish signaled the entrance of a Keeper. Bard's attention flew to the door.

Kader Calthwaite, heir of the First Line, came in with his serving boys and guards. When he was old enough, he'd take over for Chetana. It wouldn't be long now. Kader looked like a man in the ornate brown and blue leather tunic he wore. When had he gotten so old?

Soon, Haved Ganesha strode in with little Telly, who looked absurdly formal in furs. Bard's mouth twitched. Haved herself was a vision, as always, as Jori would have said.

Where was he?

As though on cue, the main double doors opened and the announcement rang the entrance of Jori, whose gaze immediately found Bard on the dais. He looked impeccable, tall and regal in a dark purple vest dotted with a green flower design. He wore a sword at his hip for some reason. It would make it more difficult to sit during the ceremony or dance afterward, but it gave him such a dashing air that it didn't matter.

Jori raised an eyebrow at Bard, who communicated back with his own facial contortions. *Yes, this is grand, and you look good too.* An honest little smirk crossed Jori's face, just as an important-looking stranger captured his shoulder and his attention.

Bard exhaled, just as the memory of Herne came back to him again. By rights, the Amir should be here too. Bard swallowed the thickness in his throat.

It was almost time.

What a strange mix of past and present it was, but then, weren't all weddings like that?

The music shifted, quieted, and the guests—old and young, royal and common, Tanyu and Amir—sat in their respective seats by the riot of blue flowers and length of silky blue fabric. Jori sat in front.

A hush fell. Bard's gut tightened with anticipation.

Lyras, drums, and pipes burst forth in loud song. At the same moment, the doors at the side of the Main opened wide to reveal Firian and Kiria, arm in arm, beaming so wide they transfigured the room with magic. A jolt of joy shot through Bard as he stood holding the pole on the platform. His eyes prickled.

Kiria stole everyone's attention first. She radiated such perfect beauty and happiness that it suddenly felt as though all things were possible, that the promise of dawn after a dark night would always come through, and that death didn't have the final word. This was realer, somehow. Her facial scars only served to enhance the feeling. Why couldn't the whole Kingdom see this moment? Then they would know their problems would be all right in the end. Their worries didn't need to consume them.

Something in Bard's mind rang with recognition.

Do not submit to fear, which pretends immortality. Its life is not as long as a single star.

Beside Kiria, Firian smiled. Really smiled. He didn't wear his Tanyuin uniform today, but instead a crisp white shirt and dark blue vest with a Kingdom pattern embroidered in gold.

Along the silken waterway they came, moving eagerly. Kiria's skirt seemed made of water. The blue fabric flowed behind her, cool and liquid. The top part floated too, soft, intricate material that twisted over her bare shoulders. One clawed point of the Keeper tattoo hooked into sight near the arrow scar on her shoulder. She wore her crown.

As they approached the platform, passing the chairs and becoming absorbed among the abundance of flowers, Bard noticed Jori smiling lopsidedly and whispering to Haved, who sat next to him. They seemed to share a secret memory, nodding and blinking rapidly to clear the welling tears. Jori tossed his head in the general direction of the musicians before returning his attention to the couple.

Firian and Kiria reached the platform and stood under the gauzy blue and white fabric held aloft by Bard and Daelon. The weight of the honor he'd been given, despite failing to qualify as an Amir, filled his chest, along with much of Firian's joy. Through their connection he'd felt fear, pain, and anger, but never delight as pure as he felt now. It welled like a fountain, merging with his own happiness at seeing them together.

The music died away and Chetana, standing before the resplendent couple, began the ceremony with a recitation song. Kiria's fingers tightened on Firian's arm as they both knelt. She looked at Chetana and he looked at Kiria. A smile played on Kiria's lips, so she knew full well that Firian was staring. The light through the canopy gilded them as though they were underwater. The stage smelled watery and green from the flowers.

When the song ended, the two of them stood. Attendants marched up the steps to commandeer the poles Bard and Daelon carried. Bard's palms were sweaty. He rubbed them surreptitiously on his trousers before joining hands with Firian first, then Chetana, who reached for her son Daelon, who completed the circle with Kiria. Firian got Bard's stiff hand so Firian had to maneuver around the unmoving fingers, but he did so seamlessly. A curious warmth filled Bard's chest.

Almost perfect.

He glanced at the foot of the dais.

Chetana and then Daelon and then Bard took turns reciting

part of the vows that Firian and Kiria confirmed. This was more than a wedding of two. It was a nation. It was a family. Bard squeezed Firian's hand before they all let go. Firian seemed to realize he was there and cast him a look—no words from the Unreal, just a quiet, grateful, familial look.

The ceremony concluded after more tradition, more recitation, mostly given by Chetana. Firian and Kiria stood close enough to each other that the clasped hands were squeezed between them. Finally, the informal part began. The audience stood, roaring their approval, or at least joining in with those who did approve of this controversial alliance. Someone took away the chairs and everyone on the platform swept down into the sea of lily petals below. Joyous music stuck up from the band.

Bard sidled up to where Jori talked to Haved and hugged him round the waist. He felt warm and cozy, and Bard just wanted to stay like that.

"What is this?" Jori exclaimed, pulling away and holding up Bard's hand. He pulled down the sleeve, exposing a black cloth underneath. "This isn't a funeral, darling."

"I know." Bard took his hand out of Jori's grasp and shoved the dark gray sleeve back again. It still felt right to wear the cloth, as though a part of the Amir were there with him. At that moment, he didn't feel sad, but he didn't want to take the mourning cloth off his wrist either.

Jori swept him off to the side just out of earshot of everyone else. Over Jori's shoulder, Bard could see Firian and Kiria coming off the dais, beaming. "Are you really all right?" he asked in an undertone.

"Yeah." Bard nodded dismissively. "I'm okay."

Jori fixed him with that gray stare. He wanted to hear the truth, even if it made things awkward. Jori never seemed to feel awkwardness, but Bard did, and this wasn't Bard's moment to steal attention with revealing conversations.

"I'm okay," he repeated. Jori didn't relent, so he lowered his voice to a whisper. "Since you're not letting up, I wish I were more like them." He didn't need to clarify which *them*. "But not... not really. Just today. I'm not sure what I mean, you know? I can still have a good time."

"They're magnificent human beings, particularly Kiria. She outshines him like the sun. But, neither one is for me. Ultimately, it was your hugs that helped me decide. There was no way I could go without those. Had to let them down easy. Ah!" Jori cried, spotting something and moving past Bard.

He spun to see Jori plant a kiss on Kiria's cheek. The couple had moved around them to say hello to Haved when Bard wasn't paying attention.

Bard's thoughts were still a tangle, and he didn't know why he'd confessed what he did, but the message hidden in Jori's words warmed his insides. Bard didn't have to want or be something more, something different. He made a mental note to tell Jori later all the reasons that he'd chosen him too.

"Why didn't you tell me about the music?" Jori asked.

"I changed it a little," Kiria said, "and I didn't want you to get your hopes up."

When Bard quirked a brow, she explained. "It was the song Atty wrote for Haved."

Jori whirled back around. "I forgot! You weren't here yet. Well, it was lovely." He cleared his throat. "Anyway, there's a point to music. Firian's a hopeless dancer so I need to teach him a few moves."

Beside Kiria, Firian leveled a look at Jori that said he took the comment as a challenge.

"We do have to stay for a while, talk to dignitaries, enjoy the party," Kiria told him in a quiet voice.

"I know. I said I'd stay. I'm timing it." He bent and kissed her neck.

"Dancing," she declared primly, straightening.

"Dancing," said Jori.

The beat had wriggled into Bard's mind, and he realized he was already bobbing to the tune. He stopped when Jori winked him, but then he grinned. "Dancing," he echoed.

"Come on, then." Jori flung himself forward, beckoning the others to follow. Even Haved joined them in the middle of the tiled floor.

They faced each other in a circle, the five of them. Kiria twirled under Firian's arm, and the rhythm took them all.

Haved's fingers tapped together curiously—one two, one two three—as she listened to the music, her square jaw tilted up in concentration. One two. One two three. She started nodding in time with the beat. For a few seconds, she and Bard were in sync. Then she raised her long skirt to reveal golden slippers beneath.

Everyone stopped to watch. She kicked and hopped and shuffled in an intricate pattern, subtle but obviously well practiced.

Jori whooped. "Do it again, love. That's marvelous!"

Haved's mouth curved upward as she repeated the steps. As soon as she finished, Jori and Kiria tried to replicate what she had done. Kiria nearly fell over, laughing. Jori, jumping higher than either of the girls had, copied Haved with a little more success. He finished the last sloppy step with a flourish and eyed Firian meaningfully in a dare.

Firian gave a curt nod and waved for Haved to demonstrate one more time. His eyes followed her every move, paying no heed to Jori, who kept cracking his knuckles telling him to get ready.

Once done, Haved met Firian's gaze and one of her dark eyebrows cocked slightly. She was challenging him too.

Firian drew his shoulders back and danced. It wasn't perfect, but the steps were more precise than Jori's and certainly Kiria's had been.

"It would be ungracious of me to take my rightful win," said Jori, pressing a hand to his chest after Firian's performance. "On your wedding day, I must concede to you." His expression was the most diplomatic one he had.

"Firian was better," Bard said.

"Oh!" Kiria exclaimed, giving Firian a quick kiss. "And Bard is the most truthful of us."

"Except for you," Firian corrected. They looked into each other's eyes long enough that it was clear the rest of them had faded far into the background.

Bard's attention wandered back to Jori, who wasn't offended. In fact, his gray eyes grew almost serious as he looked back. The moment stretched, the empty air a conversation of unspoken words.

A new song broke the spell. This one raced along its melody faster than the last. Bard's heart matched pace. The stiff collar tapped his stubbly jaw as he jumped and spun. A laugh burst out of him.

The others danced too, wildly, with no choreography, just letting the sounds and the lights and the warmth and the sparkling energy take them.

Kiria's wide grin mirrored Bard's own in the swirl of movement. Firian, attached so closely to both of them through their *katahs*, soon smiled too, broad and honest.

Then they were all laughing and dancing, every one, and the moment stood looking at itself with approval, like the ghosts of those with them.

At that moment, as they danced together, and ever after, joy was just as real as pain.

ACKNOWLEDGMENTS

Letting go of the Tanyuin Academy was difficult. I fell in love with Bard and Kiria and Firian and Chetana and Jori and all the rest. So these extra stories were born.

A huge thank you to Amanda, Debbie, Ed, Caitlyn, Quinn, Rachel, and Deborah. Your frank feedback helped this little collection ring true to the characters and their varied lives in ways I couldn't have done on my own.

ALSO BY CARLY STEVENS

The Tanyuin Academy Series

Firian Rising

Into the Unreal

Kingdoms on Fire

ABOUT THE AUTHOR

Carly Stevens lives and works as an English teacher in Colorado. She enjoys writing adventure-filled fantasy novels about courage and hope.

To find out more about upcoming projects, check out her website: www.carly-stevens.com
Her author newsletter is the best place to get an exclusive, behind-the-scenes look at the world of the Tanyuin Academy. You might even win free books for signing up!